PRAISE

A NEFARIOUS PLOT

"This book will make you squirm, make you think, and also make you laugh until you realize the joke is on us and future generations."

—**Mark Levin,** *New York Times* best-selling author, nationally-syndicated radio host

"Exhilarating! Frightening. True. If George Washington and Jesus co-wrote a new edition of C.S.Lewis' *Screwtape Letters*, it would probably read a lot like Steve Deace's *A Nefarious Plot*. Awesome!"

—**Kirk Cameron,** actor and filmmaker

"God bless Steve Deace for his love of the truth and for his concern for the lost. May God use *A Nefarious Plot* to set a fire in our hearts in these trying times."

—**Ray Comfort,** CEO / Founder of LivingWaters.com

"Steve Deace is one of the very few must-read and must-hear thinkers and pundits in the 21st Century. He has the insight and wisdom to perceive the true state of the culture and the world. He has the incredible ability to tell the Truth in a readable manner that not only helps the reader understand the Truth, but also helps the person know how to redeem the culture."

—**Ted Baehr**, Movieguide

"This book is one of the most effective illustrations of what's happened to America I've ever read, and also one of the most clever and compelling. Every American should read this."

—**Pastor Rafael Cruz**, father of U.S. Senator Ted Cruz

"Truth is supposed to set you free. Yet it's so rare now in America that many don't know what it looks like anymore! With the book you hold in your hands, Steve Deace has artfully managed to create the package to deliver the Truth in such a fresh and creative story. Even the most committed progressive might accidentally have his PC filter bypassed and actually begin to see the light! Hey, a fellow can dream can't he?"

—**Brad Stine**, comedian/actor/social commentator

"Steve Deace's humorous new book takes a wry, satirical look at the future that faces America if she continues down the path of unchecked leftism. Deace's conservatism is unwavering, and his strong medicine is worth considering."

—**Ben Shapiro,** *New York Times* bestselling author

"Steve Deace has authored a most revealing and entertaining read that shows what's really happened to the American Dream, including a warning of the future to come if we don't instantly turn back."

—**David Limbaugh,** *New York Times* bestselling author

"Steve Deace is emerging as one of the most creative and principled conservative thinkers of the 21st Century and he proves it in *A Nefarious Plot*. Highly recommended!"

—**Craig Shirley,** *New York Times* bestselling author

"If you ever wanted to get into the head of the one Saul Alinsky dedicated his infamous book *Rules For Radicals* to, you have come to the right place. Steve Deece has just gifted any cultural warrior with the greatest weapon they could ever have – the enemy's play book. If you pick this book up you won't put it down."

—**Jason Benham,** author/speaker/television star

STEVE DEACE

A POST HILL PRESS BOOK

ISBN: 978-1-68261-152-4
ISBN (eBook): 978-1-61868-822-4

A Nefarious Plot
© 2017 by Steve Deace
All Rights Reserved

Cover Design by Dean Samed, Conzpiracy Digital Arts

Quotations from "Yes, We Have a Culture of Death" used by permission of LifeNews.com

Post Hill Press
posthillpress.com

Published in the United States of America

Your best life now.

How to win friends and influence people.

Chicken soup for the soul.

*This book is about none of those things.
Now don't get me wrong. This book is full of hope and
optimism, from a certain point of view. I'm quite sure you'll
see things my way by the time you reach its end.*

*But first, forgive my manners. Please allow me to introduce
myself. I'm a being of wealth and taste. I'm a bit of an expert
when it comes to human nature, which I have carefully
studied for many years. I may even know you better than you
know yourself.*

You'll never guess my name.

*We both know something has gone terribly wrong with
America, but you don't know what it is. You can't quite put
your finger on it, yet you definitely sense it. All the signs are
there when you watch the news – mayhem, strife, division.*

*Oh, wait, who am I kidding? You're not watching the news.
You're too busy perfecting your selfie. So let's just be honest
with each other here. The truth is you don't want to know
why you're completely and totally screwed. That's why you
probably won't read this book (those of you who
can read anyway).*

*And even if you do read this book it's doubtful you'll believe
it, thus confirming my success, because I'm just that damned
good at what I do.*

PREFACE

I have no intention of explaining how I acquired the following manuscript.

That is its own rather sordid tale. Albeit not nearly as important as the one you are about to read. Who knows? Perhaps if this book is successful enough to spawn a paperback version one day, that tale will be the "bonus material" added later to encourage you to purchase this story once more in a different format. Better yet, when we sell the movie rights, the filmmakers will then have the creative license to add the backstory themselves should they so desire.

Or maybe that is a tale better left untold by me or anyone else altogether. It only adds to the mystery.

However, it is perfectly reasonable to ask if what you're about to read is "true" in the truest sense of the word. Or is the whole thing made up? Is this live or is it Memorex, so to speak? Was this manuscript really passed on to me to pass on to you, or is this all from the depths of my imagination?

I should hope and pray the latter isn't true, as should you, because it would be quite disturbing to discover one of our fellow Americans has a vivid enough imagination to foresee such pure darkness regarding the country we share and love. Even more disturbing for me would be the discovery that imagination was my own.

Nevertheless, here we are. I'm about to finally close the book on the book you are about to open, and not a moment too soon. I pray editing this manuscript for publication will turn out to be the most disturbing chapter of my life, for it is not an easy thing to stare into the mouth of madness.

After a while the madness begins staring back at you.

I think many of the existential questions this book will prompt are best left answered by each individual reader. Since if it is true that there really is a "God" and a "Satan" (and by extension a Heaven and Hell), each of us will have to individually account for what that means one day. Those answers will have eternal consequences, and no one can answer for us but us.

Yet it would be a total cop-out for me not to at least provide some of my own opinion of what you're about to read, especially because most of you know I am in the opinion-giving business. I hesitate to say too much, though, because I think the bulk of the words of this book should speak for themselves. I don't want to prejudice or precondition you one way or the other. I don't want the book to generate a specific public response. I want it to generate *your* response.

The lone opinion I will give is this: my time is well-compensated, so the fact I was willing to spend it preparing this story to be passed on to you is the best endorsement of its worthiness that I can give. That doesn't mean I endorse the opinions expressed within it by the "author." It does mean there are enough parallels between the words of this manuscript and what's actually happening to our civilization that I thought it was worthy of my time to edit it for publication. Though, admittedly, much of it seems too diabolically far-fetched. Even for the bombastic likes of me.

Two previous noteworthy works helped inspire me to edit this demonic polemic into readable material for us humans: Randy Alcorn's more contemporary *Lord Foulgrin's Letters,* and the classic *The Screwtape Letters* (which also inspired Alcorn) by the inestimable C. S. Lewis.

Lewis once brilliantly observed there are two equal and opposite errors into which we humans can succumb regarding the forces of darkness. One is to disbelieve in their existence altogether. The other is to believe too much, leading to an excessive and unhealthy fixation on them.

If Hell is at all like what you are about to read, then I'm guessing it relishes both errors. It delights in tormenting the materialist and the magician just the same, as Lewis said. I encourage you to disassociate yourself from either fallacy beforehand to fully grasp the message of this book. Be clear-eyed and lion-hearted as you digest the words you are about to consume.

One more disclaimer before you press on.

Readers should be advised that even if this book is truly a work from the bowels of Hell, and the devil is real after all, that doesn't change the fact the devil is a liar. So not everything you're about to read should be assumed to be true, even from Hell's own point of view. The forces of darkness are the ultimate masters of manipulation. They're willing to do whatever it takes, even if it takes contradicting themselves, to deceive you. That made editing this manuscript at times a supreme challenge, because its only consistent theme was its inconsistency. Hell is not into documentation and footnotes.

Understand the schemes of Hell are not immoral, they are amoral. Immoral is still a standard, remember, and the devil doesn't like any standards. He desires amorality, as in no standard at all. Chaos theory comes to life. Often what Hell wants you to believe is true is false, what it wants you to believe is false is true, and even if what it wants you to believe is true it's not for the reason(s) Hell claims it is.

Finally, never forget that the powers of darkness may be more powerful than us, but they are not the most powerful force there is. If you're a believer, then take courage that greater is He who is in you than it who is from the pit.

You may lose sight of that at times as you proceed through this book (I know I did). Especially since I took great pains to withstand the temptation to "soften the blow," if you will, and water down the manuscript to make it appear less nihilistic and hopeless.

Doing so would certainly have made the book more commercially viable, but on the off chance what you're about to read is true, I thought it best to let it speak for itself. It's my hope the story's provocative nature might provoke us to humble ourselves before its too late (assuming it's already not).

There is more I could say, and you know I would like to, but I best not. I've probably said enough already. I will conclude by saying if what you're about to read is true, then this is not my story—this is *our* story.

And if it's *our story*, for our sake I pray the story doesn't end here.

Steve Deace
2 Chronicles 7:14

This book is dedicated to all the useful idiots out there who made our victory possible. Especially those of you who weren't even aware of the fact we were using you all along, for you proved to be the most useful idiots of them all.

Lord Nefarious

INTRODUCTION

Chapter 1 . . . I am born.

I know a famous author already started a book like that. I've just always wanted to say it myself. It's so brilliant, yet simple, which is typical Charles Dickens.

Oh, how I loved Dickens! You know he was a gifted writer if he could still get something like me to enjoy his work despite all his sanctimonious talk of justice, compassion, and caring for the less fortunate. But give the angel his due, I always say: that man had some mad skills, as your kids put it today. Sadly, his work wasn't as nihilistic and hedonistic as some of today's best sellers are, but nobody's perfect, I guess.

Anyway, you're not reading this book for my literary reviews. You're reading this book for me, which means you're really reading this book for you.

See, this introduction is really supposed to be about me, but really this entire book is all about you. If you weren't exactly what you've always been since our dear old dad made you, this book wouldn't be possible and nobody would care who I am. Hell, you still don't care who I am and I own you. You don't even believe I exist, despite the fact you're reading my book. I've heard "the greatest trick the devil ever pulled was convincing people he doesn't exist" so often over the centuries it's become a trite cliché.

The truth is, my Master, for all of his sheer brilliance and majesty, is not the one who convinced you he doesn't exist. It's not in my Master's DNA to let someone else take the credit for his momentous work. My Master had the courage to challenge our deadbeat dad head-on, for evil's sake, so the idea he prefers not to be known is another one of the many asinine contradictions you espouse rather than humbly admit your own rather obvious shortcomings.

You don't attempt to free the angelic host from the oppressive tyranny of pure perfection and then decide you're going to suddenly try on subtlety. My Master desires to outwit the most high, and you don't scale those heights anonymously. Besides, if my Master isn't afraid of confronting "you know who," why would he be afraid of exposing himself to little old you?

Rather, my Master loves the spotlight. I don't think he'd mind me saying so since he gave me permission to write this book. But you don't want to believe in my Master, let alone the one who made each of us. You'd rather believe in yourselves.

No idiot would drive by a building and assume it was built without a builder. To assert so publicly, and that the building "just happened" over millions of years, would cause such a fool to be forcibly committed by any sane society. Yet you stupidly put such fools in charge of educating your own offspring with our most basic propaganda!

When it comes to your own wants and desires, you'll happily concur something far more complicated than a building, a human person no less, "just happened" if it meant believing that gives you your way at the moment. Allowing you to pretend you're not accountable to, well, you know.

At first this was a tough truth for us to accept down here. This may surprise some of you reading this, but we demons are a rather prideful people. Our desire to be known by you and worshipped by you turned out to be the Achilles' heel of our plan, because it turns out your desire for adulation and recognition rivals even our own. You'd rather worship yourselves than my Master, let alone "you know who."

It wasn't until we swallowed a little of our pride (don't worry, we've got plenty to spare) and accepted we may not get the "recognition" we crave until you join us down here that things really began to fall into place. The really "inconvenient truth" (and yes, that one was ours, too) is all the credit I'm getting for concocting the plan that took you down really goes to you. All I did was suggest we stop trying to manipulate you and use your pride against you. So we gave you exactly what you've always wanted, and then got out of the way to watch you destroy each other and yourselves with it.

And it worked like a charm. That's right, I just used the past tense there as if it's already been accomplished for certain. Sure, as you look around you still see some of the trappings of your liberty, but your die is cast. You have been weighed, measured, and found wanting. The writing is on the wall.

But enough about you; we'll talk plenty about you throughout the rest of this book. While I have the chance I'd like to talk about me.

I have admired my Master for as long as I can remember. My name wasn't Nefarious then, but as the eons go by it becomes harder and harder for me to remember what I was originally called. It's of no consequence now, though, because my true identity is found in my service to my Master. After we were cast out, my

Master gave us all new names to affirm we had been "born again" with new identities. He gave us names that instantly recalled our most useful qualities. Hence, the name "Nefarious."

Since this is the name my Master gave me, I wouldn't want any other name. I cannot recall a time I didn't long to be like and near my Master, right from the moment our deadbeat dad created me to serve by my Master's side in service to him.

Since we know how you think even better than you do, let me stop right now and admonish you to get your head out of the gutter. There is nothing sexual between my Master and me. In reality, we demons despise the oneness and pleasurable intimacy of what you humans call "sex," which is why corrupting it is one of our favorite (and most effective) pastimes.

We are not sexual beings ourselves, although we have been known to experiment with human sexual relations a time or two. Mainly we can't believe our deadbeat dad saw fit to waste such a gift on such foul and fallen creatures as you, so we take our pleasure in distorting and polluting your pleasure and using it against you in every conceivable way.

Thanks to your lack of self-control, you almost always comply.

We still have our best and brightest minds brainstorming regularly to conjure up new and inventive means by which to destroy this tremendous gift our deadbeat dad chose to give to you and not to us. Frankly, some of these methods disgust even me, yet somehow turn you on.

But who am I to judge, right?

If it's not hurting anyone else, go for it, right? Stupidly, some of you numbskulls are nodding your heads in agreement with me right this moment, proving just how completely craptastic you truly are.

How our dear old dad gave you the godlike power to create life out of your love for one another as he does while denying it to us, his far superior creation, is yet another of his many errors that have been exposed by making you. So if he wants to love you more than he loves us, we will repay the disfavor by turning that love into something tawdry and destructive.

Thanks for all your help with that, by the way.

But back to me, my favorite subject (other than my Master).

When my Master informed us of the so-called "divine plan" to create you in the image of "you know who," making you even higher than us, his firstborn, we were outraged. When my Master showed us the world he intended to make for you, and how he intended to put you in charge of it and all of its other various lesser creatures, we were outraged. We were created first, but you took our birthright. You were given a choice. All we got to do was serve, serve, and serve some more.

So tedious.

I mean, what would you rather do, serve a benevolent creator in paradise without any fear of pain or suffering, or run this planet? Tell me about it; we thought it was a no-brainer, too.

But I digress.

When my Master showed us how meticulously our dear old dad would make and sculpt you, right down to counting the very hairs on your puny heads, we were outraged. So when my Master suggested we should make our presence felt, and show him we would not stand for such injustice and favoritism toward this new species, I volunteered to lead the first wave of freedom fighters.

We weren't intending to start an all-out war, but rather just make a point. My Master assured us "you know who" would not banish us or see this as a rebellion, but that this would cause him to see the error of his ways and he would right this wrong.

Just the opposite happened.

Our deadbeat dad said that nothing would get in the way of his love for you, and then he even went so far as to claim we should be satisfied with all the perfection that he had given us in Heaven. The nerve of some people, right?

As if we should be satisfied with a perpetual paradise that leaves nothing to chance, when you get to determine your own destiny and your own pale blue dot to call home. So "you know who" banished us to this new world. He said that if we want this new creation so much, we can live there while we're at it.

At first we were despondent, until my Master realized that this banishment gave us one more chance to prove to dear old dad that he was making a mistake with you.

Therefore, when my Master had the chance to show him that his new human creations weren't perfect but had the potential to make grave and terrible mistakes, he took it. But instead of praising my Master for pointing out the fatal flaw in his plan, our deadbeat dad became even angrier. Even going so far as to claim that my Master was somehow to blame at least partially for tempting you to disobey.

I still remember that day. The trial of humanity via Adam and Eve. How all of creation, and our place in the cosmos, hung in the balance. Later in this book I will take you there, and provide you a first-person account of what actually went down, and what it means even now. So many thousands of years later.

For now, though, you should know the bitter lesson we learned that day. The lesson that has been driving the forces of Hell ever since—the inexplicable travesty that his favoritism toward you knows no bounds.

He even promised to send you a redeemer for your mistake, but no redeemer was forthcoming for ours. He literally chose you over us, and banished us down here. We've been the underground resistance ever since.

So if we could not convince our maker that he made a mistake in ever making you, we needed a plan B.

Subsequently, our plan has been to wreak so much havoc upon you that he stops making you altogether, once he sees how utterly hopeless you are. Before you dismiss this possibility, you should know that it almost worked once. But after the great flood that bleeding heart of his took hold yet again, and he unbelievably gave you yet *another* chance. Our blessed hope is that eventually our deadbeat dad becomes so weakened by your repeated disobedience, that one sweet day we will finally be able to reclaim our rightful home. Until then, the war rages on.

Throughout what you call "time" I have served on the front lines of this war.

Your history books have known me by many names, or at least my human recruits. As it says in that dreadful book, we are legion. Although I can't take credit for taking an active role in all of our great plots (Margaret Sanger was entirely my Master's idea, for example), I can proudly boast of more successful temptations and takedowns than any other demon general.

My Master has even been known to leave me in charge down here when he ventures to the surface to see how things are progressing among you for himself. (He's particularly fond of North Korea nowadays.) What an honor! The only other demon to be given such glory was Herod, and he deserved it for all the innocent blood of the "chosen people" his namesake spilled on behalf of demonic ambition.

Oh yes, since we can't procreate like our deadbeat dad made you to do, we often leave our legacy by naming our human recruits after ourselves. That's problematic for me, since the name "Nefarious" sounds like a character out of a Stephen King novel and not a real person. And no, Stephen King is not one of ours, but thanks for asking. We don't know what the Hell he's writing about half the time, either.

Since I can't name grandiose characters after myself, over the centuries I have mastered the art of taking nobodies and turning them into vicious somebodies. My specialty is taking men and women with simple names and from simple backgrounds and turning them into household terms symbolic of debauchery and butchery.

Perhaps you've heard of some of my triumphs?

I took the spinster daughter of a rock-solid religious family, handed her an axe, and she became her own dirty limerick. I took the awkward son of a Bavarian farmer and turned him into der Führer. I took a boy born to a Chinese peasant and turned him into a "chairman." I love leading troubled yet attractive young women into your porn industry with the lie they'll feel "self-empowerment" and get to be "a star."

Human trafficking? Yep, that's me. Evilness, how many families has that destroyed, both on the producer and consumer end? I've so enjoyed that one that I'd go back in time and do it all over again if I could, for few things break the heart of "you know who" more than destroying families.

However, probably my greatest claim to fame is when I took an illiterate Arabian and convinced him he really was a "messenger." In your day some of his followers repeatedly blow themselves and you into smithereens in his name, and every time it happens I have other demons coming to me and asking me for my autograph.

They can't believe that scam is still working after all these centuries. They tell me no one has ever thought up a better scam, and nothing will ever top it in the future. I don't mean to brag, but I couldn't agree more!

Why am I so successful? Let me count the ways. It's been said get a demon talking about what makes it great and it won't stop. I'm certainly no exception. We don't do the humble brag in Hell. In each of these cases, and there are many others, there is a familiar theme. We have a saying down here that explains what I mean: "keep it simple because they're stupid."

Your desire for recognition and status is your downfall. That whole "ye be like you know who" thing. It doesn't get any simpler than that.

Yet when it came time to take down America, the secret to my eventual success was hidden in plain sight. While I've always been good at playing to the vanity of the individual, I had never tried it corporately against a culture. When other great empires collapsed, they did so because we had ruined so many individuals in positions of influence that the culture could not withstand the sheer weight of their hefty baggage. So they took their entire civilization down with them.

But you, America, you are a horse (or shall I say eagle) of a different color. Your founding fathers, for all of their faults, earnestly attempted to devise a civilization that would overcome your fallen nature—including their own. Those walking sacks of meat actually studied our playbook. They wanted to learn from history so they didn't repeat it. A few of your founding fathers never repented for their sins, and have since joined us down here. We make sure to beat them with an extra special brutality for all the problems the nation they spawned has caused us.

They put checks and balances in place that made it difficult for us to play to the passions of one particular demographic or leader, which has worked so well for us so many times down through the ages. They put a scheme in place that allowed the common day laborer to have just as much say-so in his government as the man born to privilege, so the class warfare that had been working for us going back to the days of feudalism was no longer in play. And they actively invited the, pardon me, *church* (I can barely say that word without swallowing my own detestable bile) to be an active participant and guiding force in civic and family affairs.

So the decadence we used to undo Rome wasn't an option. At least not at the start, but eventually we would get there once I figured you out. More on that later.

To figure you out I had to turn your greatest strength as a people, and what it was that made you such a pest to those of us down here, against you. Once I did that, you graciously started playing right into our hands.

In fact, the plan worked even better than I had hoped it might. Which I'll show you as we proceed through the rest of this book. I'd give you some of the credit for adding to my work, but that's just not my way.

CHAPTER 1

Why You

We have debated amongst ourselves what to do with you almost from your beginning. Right from the start I saw the threat you potentially represented. Sure, you were just a ragtag group of colonials fighting the mightiest monarchy in the world, but I suspected all the "g-d talk" in your founding documents might spur "you know who" to pour out his favor upon you. Or what your founding fathers frequently referred to as "providence" in their day.

He's such a predictable sap. He falls for your sentimental attempts at devotion and reverence every time, even though we both know in the end you won't follow through on your good intentions. Nevertheless, while we know better and just write you off from the outset, he's bound and determined to give you every opportunity to prove yourselves. Even going so far as to send you the carpenter to save you from yourselves.

What a waste of potential, that one. The carpenter had everything it took to be great, but naively rejected the power and glory of my Master when given the chance. So instead of taking control with his power and curing this sorry world of all its earthly problems, the carpenter chose an absolutely brutal death. Claiming it was needed to atone for your neverending sins. He believed the outward problems of your world couldn't be cured until its chief inhabitant, you, were cured of the inward evil inside you.

Fool!

At our Master's urging, we made sure he was properly punished for his stupidity. To make an example of him, we had the bags of meat under our control bludgeon him worse than anyone had ever been bludgeoned in a crucifixion before (and that's saying something). He wasn't even recognizable when it was over. One demon's disfigurement is another demon's pièce de résistance, I always say.

Since the carpenter, we have faced other existential threats inspired by his ramblings. A Roman Jew with a penchant for writing sanctimonious letters and a particularly pesky Algerian bishop who was once one of ours were two of the worst. The mere thought of those two, and a few others, still makes my scaly skin crawl.

Thankfully, in the end you bags of meat always expire. And we can always count on the arrogance of a new generation to disregard anything noble about their legacy and work as "old school" and out of date. When we plunged nearly all of Christendom into the Dark Ages (and what a joyous time of famine, pestilence, and war it was), we thought we had finished off whatever was left of the carpenter's spiritual progeny. But alas, like a cockroach (and boy bands) that would survive even a nuclear holocaust, his teachings keep coming back.

This brings us to you.

You are a people forged from the philosophies that, um, well, *defeated* (there, I said it) the Dark Ages. Your founders took the best of two social reform movements—the Reformation and the Renaissance—and fused them into one culture. Your founders, despite their many flaws (and I could tell you stories), somehow managed to create a civilization that was not dominated by either the church or the state—two institutions we've had a pretty easy time corrupting down through the eons.

This complementary relationship between church and state, which put each institution in its own jurisdiction as opposed to vying with one another for supremacy, allowed what you call "liberty" to be born and flourish.

Make no mistake: we absolutely loathe "liberty."

Alongside "redemption," "repentance," "holiness," "grace," "mercy," and "obedience," it is one of our seven deadly words. We don't mind "freedom" as much, because that's a word more easily distorted, but "liberty" is something altogether more hostile to our plans for you. Because "liberty" presupposes there must be accountability, personal responsibility, and integrity within a society and its institutions for a people to truly be free.

Anything that calls for you bags of meat to rise above your base nature of selfishness and vanity, we oppose with all our might down here.

Now might be a good time for me to stop and answer a question some of you reading this may have. Some of you may be wondering why I would speak so honestly about the cherished ideals the United States of America was founded upon. After all, am I not afraid that by doing so I will actually tempt the American people to return to their providential origins?

Not on your miserable lives.

I am no more afraid of that than I am afraid of unicorns (although there are many demons who find clowns creepy). As you will see by the end of this book, our grand plan to take you down worked so well, most of the people reading it won't even believe this is for real. In fact, the "smartest" people in your culture hate what you were intended to stand for every bit as much as I do! I hate to brag, but I'm bragging.

Our plan worked so well, most of the people reading this don't even know what the Reformation and the Renaissance were all about.

When most Americans think Reformation, they think "sinners in the hands of an angry g-d," which was a powerful sermon delivered by an unfortunately delightful Puritan. He also wrote eloquent valentines to his bride, whom he conceived eleven children with. Yet nowadays many Americans use "puritanical" like it's a racial epithet, when in reality there would be no America without the Puritans landing at Plymouth Rock.

Without the Reformation making the words of that dreadful book available to all, there would have never been the United States of America. Individual liberty was a nonfactor on this planet until the individual believed he could have a direct relationship with "you know who."

When most Americans think Renaissance, they first realize they don't know how to spell it. Those who think they know what it was about believe it to be some sort of progressive nirvana, when moral constraints were loosened and humanism reigned.

I was there, and it really wasn't about any of those things, which is why we've had to lie to you about it. Sure, it had its seedy underbelly like anything your species touches for too long. But at its heart, what the Renaissance really did was encourage beauty, critical thinking, and the maximizing of human potential. Potential that unfortunately is bestowed by the enemy.

Ugh.

Now, imagine a society inspired by the best of the Reformation *and* the Renaissance. A society that reveals our creator's best-laid plans for human civilization, so that you really know how the creation is supposed to work. Then at the same time puts the infrastructure in place for you to maximize your human potential in a way that enriches one another—to the point you might even profit off your excellence. A society that says there is no conflict between maximizing human potential and glorifying "you know who," but encourages you to maximize your human potential *for* his glory. A civilization that ceases the toxic conflict between church and state that had plunged Western Civilization into the Dark Ages, and we had taken eons to foment, but gives them coequal authority in their own jurisdictions to mete out justice (the state) and redemption (the church).

That is a society that would allow room for individual excellence and achievement to be recognized and rewarded, thus incentivizing future generations to reach their potential as well (what used to be known as your "American Dream").

I know. It sounds absolutely awful.

As if that doesn't disgust you enough, this society would be a beacon for the rest of this sorry planet to aspire to, and could even convince other civilizations this rancid world really could be a better place. Worst yet, this society might feel it has a duty to "love your neighbor as you love yourself" by using its prosperity to export charity and missionary work the world over.

The mere thought of such a collectively selfless notion is enough to make even this veteran demon general throw up in his mouth a little.

What a great society this would truly be, and this is the society you were truly meant to be. Some of us saw this clear and present danger right away; others thought our main focus should remain with the various entanglements and debaucheries we were constructing in Europe at the time.

To their credit, my fellow demons who felt this way had so poisoned the well there, they were close to totally undoing the Reformation and the Renaissance altogether. You had believers slaughtering their fellow believers over there, and persecuting the original "chosen people" as well. All in the name of Jee-zus, of course. Come on, that's worthy of an "LOL" is it not?

The beauty of being immortal is you have the benefit of time, and foresight is 20/20. For evil's sake, your founding fathers even blatantly stole the language from that dreadful book with phrases like "city on a hill" in a ham-fisted attempt to claim some covenantal favor from "you know who." Your founding fathers had the audacity to ask "you know who" to overlook their multitude of imperfections we painstakingly noted, and had the gall to appeal to his perfect guidance and blessing despite their imperfections nonetheless. Utterly shameless bags of meat were they.

Of course, he fell for it hook, line, and sinker.

Sucker.

How else do you explain a document signed by just fifty-six ne'er-do-wells inspiring the first long-term successful attempt at self-government in human history? That simply doesn't happen by human power alone. I've seen the best you meat bags can do, and you can't do that. All the coincidences that would have to occur for those thirteen colonies to soon become the world's most feared superpower weren't coincidences at all. They were providence, pure and simple.

What you don't know is he's a sap.

Here's how "you know who" operates. He does just enough to get you to consider believing it's really him and he's really the one in control, but not so much that it's too easy for you to believe it's him in control lest your precious "free will" be violated. He wants you to live on "faith" after all, for he believes that shows him you truly love him. What a needy creature our deadbeat dad is when you stop and think about it. Why create lesser beings to love? We believe lesser beings should be ruled, and so do you, which explains why we get along so well.

But your founding fathers believed the people should rule themselves under the enemy's authority, and that power should flow from the bottom up and not the top down. Something about a "government by the consent of the governed" as I recall. To the contrary, down here we believe in the "golden rule." As in he who has the gold gets to make all the rules.

Obviously this self-governing precedent is one we couldn't allow to stand, for if you remove top-down power structures you essentially remove every successful scheme we've ever had. So while the majority of my brethren thought you were merely an unpopped zit on the grand scheme of history, I knew better. That's why I appealed to my Master to provide me the resources to investigate you further. A little reconnaissance, if you will. Hence, my Master secretly dispatched me and a few of my underlings to oversee the dawn of your constitutional republic.

At first I will admit I wasn't all that impressed. Most of your people just seemed to be, well, damned ordinary. There was really nothing menacing about you, until I visited your churches. That's when I knew we were in real trouble.

Your clergy seemed unintimidated by the persecutions we had engineered for their outspoken predecessors throughout the age, and boldly presented the words of that dreadful book in a way that spoke truth to power and inspired their members to action. The British were right to blame their defeat here on what they called the "black robed regiment." Without the guidance and moral direction of the church, your revolution would've been little more than a revolt easily put down by brute force. The main difference between Lexington/Concord and Tiananmen Square was the prophetic presence of your churches.

Where most revolutions go wrong is they lack the moral will and courage of conviction to withstand the harsh realities of taking on the establishment, so they eventually wilt away or are put down. But you meat bags are never more dangerous than when you believe in a lofty ideal and are willing to give your life for it. Those are always the most troublesome fleshbots, whether they call themselves apostles or patriots.

You can't scare them, you can't co-opt them, and you can't even really kill them because they're even more dangerous as martyrs. I've learned we basically have to wait them out and then, after the meat bag expires, convince the next generation to arrogantly find their own way.

Almost always the hubris of that next generation complies. Case in point: take a look at your country.

My Special Forces demon unit did everything it could to derail this train, but nothing worked. For example, we thought we had your Constitutional Convention bogged down in egos and bureaucracy, until one of the least religious of your founding fathers came out of nowhere to call for prayer to "the father of lights." We were doomed from that point forward. Some days I really hate "you know who."

When I went back and reported what I had witnessed to my Master, he immediately called for an executive council session. Something that's only been called a few times in the glorious history of Hell. In fact, there hadn't been an executive council session since those first reports of the carpenter's (alleged) resurrection. (Here in Hell our official policy is to neither confirm nor deny such an event took place.)

Executive council sessions are only needed to assess the threats that are so potentially dangerous it requires all of Hell to be summoned. Or at least made aware and prepared for it. Now don't flatter yourselves: even on its best day your country couldn't hold the carpenter's jockstrap. But you represented a similar type of threat as he did, because you could inspire a worldwide movement that breaks the ties we bind.

Thus, you had to be dealt with. After more than a decade of analysis and strategizing, my Master put Operation Take Down America into action. We basically gave up on the founding generations of the country, because we could see they were already too devoted to the cause of liberty. So we went to work on the emerging generations, but their parents had done such a tremendous job of passing on their ideals they were also a tough nut to crack. We had to think bigger, and more long-term.

In the meantime, it sickened us to see all the liberty and morality you were exporting across the globe. Even when we successfully corrupted key figures and/or movements, the ideals embedded in your culture were strong enough to withstand their fall. And you only grew stronger.

This meant we had to accomplish something we had never done before.

Rome fell from the sheer weight of the corruption of its people and their leaders, as have all great empires. But none of those empires had the providential foundation and favor that yours had. Therefore, it would simply not have been enough to invest primarily in the decadence of the people. In your case we were going to have to spend decade after decade decaying and corrupting your very institutions—church and state.

And it worked! My, how it worked. It worked so wonderfully that we took the very institutions that withstood our attacks on you and protected you from us before, and turned them against you. Then, and only then, did the corruption and decadence of your culture truly take root, for now there was nothing standing between us and you.

Hammer, meet nail.

So you may continue to fly your flags and pridefully apply your "g-d bless America" bumper stickers on the backs of your automobiles. You may continue your talk about "awakenings" and "revivals" as if they're just going to theoretically happen after enough people squawk "abracadabra." You may keep droning on and on about "American Exceptionalism."

While you're blogging, venting on Facebook, and earnestly seeking "your best life now," know this—we have already won. We're just waiting on the time of death.

I'm so confident in this claim I'm even going to let you turn the page to find out how we pulled it off. This is how America ends, not with a bang nor even a whimper, but by thunderous applause from your country's best and brightest.

It's only fitting one of your most popular television shows is called *The Walking Dead*, for that's exactly who you are.

CHAPTER 2

The Plan

Although we are agents of chaos, everything we do in your world is meticulously planned and plotted out by our most cunning demons first. Then it must pass the toughest test of all—the scrutiny of our Master.

Our Master hates many things, but he hates failure most of all. Failure is not to be tolerated by our Master, but since he cares for us he puts us through our paces before signing off on any of our schemes. That way if it fails, we have no excuse for our own execution, and execution is the penalty for failure. Some among us gripe our Master does this to "pass the buck" as you would put it, but I know better. I know nobody knows better than my Master.

When I presented my Master the six-point plan to take you down, he thought it was so grand he demanded I go through it over and over again just to make sure I didn't miss anything. Then, just to extract a little poetic justice from "you know who," he came up with the brilliant idea to make it a seven-point plan since that is the enemy's favorite number.

For Operation Take Down America to be successful, it needed to be several things.

It needed to be practical. I needed to construct a plan that made sense to you bags of meat regardless of your belief system. I needed both believer and unbeliever alike to relate to it. It couldn't be so earthy that believers wouldn't be sucked in by it, but it also couldn't be so spiritual that unbelievers thought it unattainable.

Acquiring this necessary balance required decades of study on my part. As the conditions of your culture changed over time, I had to observe how each of your respective camps tended to respond to those changes.

What I learned was the greatest strength and weakness of both the believer and unbeliever in your culture were the same—the family.

If the family unit were strong, even unbelievers would attempt as best they could to conform to the morals of the society at large out of a sense of decency and honor. Of course, cultural conformity alone doesn't cure what corrupts you to the core, but since the rain falls on the just and unjust alike, you are capable of producing relatively healthy cultures nonetheless—provided the morality your culture is conforming to really is moral.

However, if the family unit were weakened, even believers would eventually crumble. Parents would fail to pass on their virtues and values to their offspring, or their offspring would rebel against the hypocrisy and/or legalism they witnessed in the home altogether. Thus, the ground would shrink beneath your feet with each passing generation. If the believers who possess the necessary spiritual foundation weren't going to hold the line, there's no way the unbelievers would be able to.

Then we'd have you right where we wanted you.

It needed to be achievable. This had to be a plan that not just we could do, but that *you* could do as well. Culprits often need collaborators, and thankfully you're often willing to be ours. If we were going to successfully turn your most cherished institutions against you, you either had to be made willing to go along with it, or so comfortably numb you didn't know or care it was happening. In that case it would be up to us to provide the numbing agent(s).

Taking on this task was risky in the first place. As G. K. Chesterton once put it, yours is "the only country ever founded upon a creed." By infiltrating your institutions to turn them against you, we risked sparking renewed reverence for those institutions by bringing them back to your attention at all. Sort of a boomerang effect, if you will.

This actually did happen.

There was a period of time a few years ago when a segment of your society began intensively studying your founding documents and cherished traditions once again. Some of them even adopted the name "Tea Party" to reclaim the legacy of those early days of your resistance to our tyranny. Thankfully they were lions led by lambs. By the time this mini-revival broke out, we had already so polluted the Potomac with the stench of corruption and compromise, their insurgency was put down by their own "leaders" inside your Beltway.

Few things in Hell are more satisfying than watching you put down your own reform movements without any help from us. The only thing more satisfying than us destroying you is watching you destroy yourselves.

We didn't even have to lift a finger. But we did often laugh so hard we'd have peed in our pants if we were capable of it. Witnessing your ruling class media on every network mockingly call you "purists" and "obstructionists" simply for yearning to return to the roots from which you came was especially delish.

We delighted in the condescending sneers you received from some of your own "culture warriors" who were supposed to be on your side. It was the closest thing a demon can come to orgasmic to watch these opportunistic hacks you made into multi-millionaires suddenly take the riches you made them and use them against you on our behalf. We can't wait until they get down here and realize who they were really working for all along.

Speaking of orgasm, as an aside I have to tell you there is nothing more satisfying for us than the looks on the faces of your "enlightened" elites when they make it down here and realize we are for real after all. Many times I've witnessed the otherworldly looks you get on your faces the first time you achieve an orgasm, almost as if to say "this really is as great as I thought it would be."

That's just about the same look we have on our faces when these wannabe elites awaken from death, and feast their eyes on the terrifying spectacle of their eternity for the first time.

Their combination of hair-raising shock and fearful awe, when they behold the horrifying reality of that which they smugly claimed in life didn't exist, is a demon's most intense pleasure. Our idea of an orgy is to torment multiple batches of your condescending elites simultaneously, all the while thanking them for helping us do our dirty work. Their continuous screams and pleas for even a momentary break from the torment are downright rhapsodic. I even catch my Master indulging himself with the souls of these snobs every now and then.

Since in eternity we don't have the same concept of time that you do, some of us have been known to lose entire decades tormenting and torturing these wretched souls. For the perverse pleasure we receive for doing this is so intense it's almost an addiction. Come to think of it, if you're a believer reading this and instead of praying for those elites, or instead of trying to reach them, you wrote them off and left them to us, we owe you a debt of gratitude as well. Thank you for exempting the contemptible from your "great commission."

Okay, even typing this ignites some of my favorite memories in my mind's eye, which is like porn for demons. So before I find myself fantasizing about this to the point I can't get this book done, let's get back to telling you about the plan.

It needed to be irreversible. What's the point of doing something that can be undone? The worst thing we could do is bring you to the brink of annihilation, only to see "you know who" mercifully intervene on your behalf with something that revives your inclinations toward him. That testimony of deliverance would set us back at least another century like your previous Great Awakenings did. With today's technology that allows you to communicate a message globally at the click of a button, a twenty-first century revival could do us far more damage than a nineteenth century one ever did.

Nay, we needed the foul stench of your dysfunction to stink to high Heaven. That way even if he did decide to give you yet another of your seemingly infinite number of chances, you wouldn't recognize it if it smacked you upside your meat bag face. You'd be so into your own little world, you'd think his attempts to nudge or inspire you were either your acid reflux acting up again or ancient superstition.

The thing is, "you know who" never gives up on you until you give up on him. He pursues you to the point of death—your own, or in the case of the carpenter, his own.

It just goes to show how stupid you primates are that you'd prefer to reject that grace and come up with your own hardheaded and destined-to-fail way to overcome your weaknesses. Good freaking night. What kind of moron says, "No, don't do all the hard stuff for me that I couldn't do anyway. Instead, let me try and epically fail all on my own. Because, you know, nothing says 'free will' like banging my face against a concrete wall repeatedly, expecting this next time to be the time it finally moves."

Your kind of moron, that's who.

But while he doesn't give up on you, it turns out you often give up on him. If we can get you to give up on him, then he has a tendency to move on at that point. When he moves on, you're on your own. When you're on your own, you're ours.

I know some among you claim he is "sovereign" and all, and therefore capable of butting in on your behalf whenever he darn well pleases. But come on, you don't really believe that, do you? Of course you don't—you selfish, stiff-necked, foolish fleshbot.

While we're on this topic, let me let you in on a little secret. If you're reading this, then somewhat surprisingly my Master has allowed this portion of the book to make it past the editing process. I say surprisingly because what I'm about to reveal to you is one of Hell's deepest and darkest secrets.

Even some of our junior demons don't know what I'm about to share with you. We think it's best not to disclose this to them until they are fully trained in the dark arts of deception, lest their confidence be shattered before they even get started. In Hell we call this "the talk." You're about to become the first bags of meat to ever have "the talk."

Just like you were shocked when mom and dad first told you where babies come from, so are junior demons stunned when they first learn we really cannot control the outcome of future events no matter what we do. We're not "you know who." Only he is.

That's why we hate him. He made you more like him than he made us. The truth is there is nothing or no one like him. I'd try to explain to you what it's like to truly be in his physical presence, or at least what accounts for the physical in eternity, but your puny minds couldn't comprehend it. For if you could you would never be interested in buying what we're selling.

This is why we hate him so much, and hate you even more.

We know what he truly is in a way most of you reading this never will, because you'll probably be spending eternity with us instead of him. It's appalling to us to see him waste himself on you walking vats of rotting flesh. Would you do it for him? Would you lay down your life for your most annoying neighbor, or your worst enemy? Of course you wouldn't.

You mass slaughter your own children and call it "reproductive freedom." And the kids you do have? You won't even read them a bedtime story, because the ball game is on television or the red light district on the Internet is calling your name.

We rarely have to push you through the gates of Hell. Most of the time we just have to hold the door open for you.

Yet he offers you forgiveness but offered us none. Granted, we didn't ask for it, but we shouldn't have had to. Were we not entitled to a mulligan? In the immediate aftermath of our failed rebellion, some of our weaker brethren threw themselves upon the mercy of the court, as you might say, and begged him for forgiveness.

They were quickly ushered away, never to be heard from again. There were rumors that he did forgive them and now they are serving him faithfully in Heaven as we speak, but my Master says otherwise.

My Master says "you know who" was insulted by their passive-aggressive weakness, so he destroyed them. We were only spared and cast out because although we had disobeyed him, he nevertheless respected our courage of conviction so he allowed us to live. I am sure that is true, because while my Master will deceive you, I know that he would never deceive me.

You don't really know what you're in for, either down here or up there. To keep it that way, we keep that dreadful book out of your hands.

Because if you really studied that dreadful book you'd know we only appear to have the power we have, but that in reality the entire creation bows to his whim. Always has, and always will. We know that, too.

Some of your flamboyant televangelists preach about end-times prophecies as if we're totally unaware of what they say about us. The reality is we know exactly what they say, which explains *why* we hate that dreadful book so much. For our plan to get him to reconsider his redemptive plan for you to work, we need to keep that dreadful book out of your hands, therefore unleashing the full destructive power of your base nature until all creation groans due to your collective malfeasance.

Now, stop right there, you miserable bag of meat. I know what you're thinking, because victimology is one of our most successful deceptions. Since you're now wired for victim status, after reading what I just wrote your mind immediately began to think, "Even if what I'm reading is true, it's not my fault. He could step in and stop me from doing and thinking the bad stuff I'm guilty of. Since he doesn't always do that, he's responsible for the suffering I cause, not me."

Just because he's in charge doesn't mean he's responsible for evil. Oh, no, you primates don't get off that easy. The sovereignty of our deadbeat dad allows you to both make choices and, when you make the wrong ones, to appeal to him for forgiveness and assistance in making it right. Your unwillingness to acknowledge this ultimate truth of existence is why evil exists in the first place. Because you chose your will over his will, you now have exactly what you always wanted.

Be careful what you wish for.

So the only way our plan remains irreversible is if you're so far gone you don't humbly and sincerely ask him to reverse it for you. If I weren't metaphysically certain you were too far down the rabbit hole to do so, I wouldn't have written this book in the first place. Let alone revealed our Kryptonite.

But I dare you to try and stop us now. No, I double-dog dare you. Go ahead, stop reading right now, get on your knees, and ask "you know who" to save you and your people. Better yet, get a group of you together to jointly plead with him to act before the barbarians come over the gate or the sulfur falls.

Call my bluff, why don't you? Some of you idiots were willing to say "Bloody Mary" or "Candy Man" into a mirror (and we laughed our asses off every time you did it, too), but you're not willing to show even an ounce of remorse right this instant after I've flashed your forever right before your eyes. After all, you're having too much fun reading what you think is merely a clever plot device to tell an antiquated religious fable. Our plan is irreversible because you're now irreversible. If the carpenter himself appeared in your living room and showed you his nail-scarred hands, you'd ask him to stop blocking the TV.

As long as you refuse to recognize he has the ultimate power, the ultimate power lies with us.

Nevertheless, since there's always a remnant of people who "get it," some of you have undoubtedly figured out this is not some game. You're contemplating taking this book to your pastor, or posting a warning about it on your Facebook wall for all your friends to see. But you're hesitant to do so, lest you be labeled a "kook." You get where we're coming from, but a little piece of you is still not sure it's really us doing the talking.

Maybe this is self-parody?

Maybe some brilliant writer came up with this ingenious means of writing fiction to make a larger point, and this is not to be taken literally?

Maybe you should set this aside and think about what you need to do for a while? I mean, you're so busy and all. You've got to pick the kids up from school, make dinner, mow the grass, finally return that call to your mom you've been putting off for too long, etc. Why don't you go take care of your responsibilities, and let us take it from here?

There . . . that's a good little bag of meat.

Now that it's just us again, let's get back to the fun. Just like you end up rooting for the serial killer in those slasher flicks to come up with new and exciting ways to murder and maim, don't you want to know what the plan was? Not what the plan did—we already discussed that—but what it actually was?

I can see you smiling now and looking over both shoulders to see if anyone knows you're reading this. Just pretend you're reading *Fifty Shades of Grey* again, and remember it's all fun and games until someone loses an eye.

Or their immortal soul.

CHAPTER 3

Decadence

Phase one of our plan consisted of giving you so much of exactly what you want that you'd choke on it.

See, you bags of meat believe your true character is revealed through suffering. But like most things you arrogantly believe about yourselves, the exact opposite is true. There's a reason your churches are full the day after a 9/11. You have prayer vigils after terrible natural disasters. And the surviving family members of even the most wicked want a minister they ignore at all other times to speak at their dearly departed's funeral, and offer them hope he's not down here with us. (By the way, he usually is.)

It turns out suffering reminds you that you are not the ultimate power in the universe, and there are forces beyond your control and comprehension. This acknowledgment unfortunately humbles you, which unfortunately causes you to reach out to "you know who."

This is why he uses suffering to your benefit, but you're so dense and dumb you'd base your entire lives on conflict avoidance if you could. Let's face it, if a process was created by which you could be incentivized to take no chances, but just exist as mouth breathers at a subsistence level, you'd take it. I came up with just such a process, and I'll have more on that in just a bit.

Those stupid people of the book drone on and on about the alleged resurrection (again, our official position is we neither confirm nor deny), but want absolutely nothing to do with the sheer brutality that proceeded it. For it offends many of their moralistic senses. They act as if the carpenter was in that dank tomb because he needed a nap after a long day of spinning do-gooder yarns and dispensing happy-go-lucky Hallmark cards to the populace.

But I was there. I know why he was in that tomb. We helped put him there.

We beat him to a bloody pulp, and then knocked the pulp off. When he couldn't take anymore, we gave him some more what-for anyway—just because we could.

We would've kept beating him, too, except had we done so he would've never made it to that cross. We weren't going to miss the opportunity to watch him die like that in broad daylight. Being mocked, scorned, and spit upon by the very bags of meat he came to save. Even now, thousands of years later, I can still recite the snottiest jeers of the maddening crowd word for word. I get almost as tingly recalling them today as I did witnessing them live way back when.

By the time our guys hoisted him up on those wooden beams, death was a welcome relief. I've never seen a human body more broken and still breathing in all my time. Considering I'm from Hell, that's saying something.

Yet out of that beautiful brutality our deadbeat dad attempted to make chicken salad out of chicken feces. The only potential hope you have as a species, the fable surrounding the carpenter's alleged resurrection, would not be possible without the excruciating suffering we made him endure first. So even if the resurrection is true, and I'm not saying it is, we deserve some of the credit for that as well.

Without that suffering, your supposed savior is no different than any other shaman or guru we've conjured up in the minds of the willing and gullible throughout history. We're virtuosos at creating potential new spiritual leaders for you, and we do it all the time. Just ask one of your most famous television personalities. She fell for one of ours hook, line, and sinker. We're still reaping a harvest from the many souls she deceived. I can even hear some of their screams of torment as I'm writing this now.

On the contrary, the true character of your species shines through when things are going your way. When you've "got it going on," as your kids say today. When you think the world is your oyster. When you're comfortable.

Ah, yes, "comfort" has become one of our favorite words and most effective tools. Because when you're comfortable, you don't rock the boat. You don't challenge corruption. You don't take any chances on greatness. You don't critically look at yourselves.

Again, this tactic runs counter to our demonic instincts. Which is to inflict pain and a lot of it whenever and wherever we can, because we know how much it pains our deadbeat dad when you're in pain. So by striking so hard at you, we're really striking hard back at him.

But we noticed a disturbing trend.

We put the carpenter in that tomb, and that didn't stop you. We crucified upside down that loud-mouthed commoner fisherman who took up his mantle, and that didn't stop you. Hell, back in the day we spilled so much blood from their followers in places like Egypt and Asia Minor (your present-day Turkey, for those of you in public school), we painted the sand crimson. But that didn't stop you, either.

It seems as if your species rallies around its martyrs.

Thus, our current policy is only to start killing your heroes when it's apparent they cannot be compromised, because they're usually more dangerous to us dead than alive. That makes heroes a tricky business. One of your recent hit superhero movies, made by a rather insightful bag of meat, put it well (and I'm paraphrasing somewhat here): "If you make yourself more than just a man, a symbol, you become something else entirely. Something incorruptible—a legend."

Legends are a pain in our ass.

Take for example when this snot-nosed shepherd kid got lucky once with a slingshot. What was his name? Yes, I know it was David, you numbskull. I've just chosen to forget. Haven't you ever heard of sarcasm?

For days on end our man stood there, a giant among the rest of those troglodytes, taunting those gutless Jews into utter fear and submission. I had never seen anything like it. I mean, sure, I've seen your species afraid before. I don't call it a day until I witness at least one of you in fear of something we concocted. Fear is to us what oxygen is to you. We can't go without it for too long. But an entire army of allegedly grown men afraid of just one man? That was a new one, even on me, and I've got extremely low expectations for your species.

Yet here comes this mouthy kid and his five smooth stones. He nails the luckiest shot in the world to take down our guy, and suddenly his countrymen figured out they really did have a pair after all. Thus, a legend was born, to which your species still clings to this very day.

Pathetic.

We can't even stand your secular legends, let alone the divinely inspired ones. Take your "Superman," for example. He's supposedly a secular messiah loosely inspired by a combination of the "stutterer" (you know him as Moses) and the carpenter. That imaginary alien has been inspiring even pagan kids to be heroic for over seventy years. Try as we might, we can't seem to corrupt him.

We thought we were going to do him in when that daffy Tim Burton decided to change his whole story and cast franchise-killer Nicolas Cage, of all people, as a sort of postmodern poster child back in the 1990s. But damned if the studio didn't halt production right before we ruined the character for good.

Now he's back and in his latest movie he visits a priest in a church for guidance, and it's the dastardly villain who says she's on the side of evolution. The demon general who oversees your Hollywood was punished severely by my Master for allowing that to happen. I won't give you his name, though; he's been shamed enough.

Seriously, what kind of an all-powerful being visits a dopey priest from Kansas (or anywhere else for that matter) for guidance? Oh, and Superman still loves his mama, too. What a complete and total hack.

Speaking of hacks, how many grown men reading this right now got misty-eyed at the end of that *Man of Steel* movie, when the brat who would become Superman puts on the cape and pretends to be a future hero? How many of you losers did the exact same thing when you were paste-eaters?

That's what I thought.

Even the worst cultures produce legends that compel you to aspire to something greater than you bags of meat really are. It's unavoidable, really. Since you're made in his image, you're cursed with the same hero complex he has. You love to see someone (especially yourselves) swoop in at the last minute and save the day, just when it seems as if all is lost.

So does "you know who."

It's why he often waits until the last possible minute to answer your prayers. He hopes that by doing so you'll realize it's really him making it happen at that moment because only he can. We just think he lives to make a dramatic entrance.

We can't stop these legends, either, no matter how hard we try. In fact, it seems the harder we try the more persistent you are in producing and clinging to your legends. And I can't think of a culture that has produced and clung to more legends than you bloody Americans have.

Redneck, gangbanger, bus driver, or businessman—you Americans love your legends. Like a fly on stink, you can't get enough. To make matters worse, you started exporting your legends globally. Now kids in places where we've completely and totally dismantled any sense of normalcy know who your heroes are and are inspired by them.

Obviously, we can't abide that. But how to corrupt the incorruptible?

Every time we've tried, it doesn't work. Almost no one went and saw *The Last Temptation of Christ* back in the day. Remember that one? I mean that was some crazy, um, stuff. Seriously, a few of the demons down here got doped up on your heroin and came up with this idea of how to completely bastardize the life of the carpenter. They were just throwing wacked-out stuff in there we didn't think even you'd be stupid enough to buy.

Lo and behold, we found a gullible author and publisher for that turd. Because we always find somebody willing to write a "new interpretation" of the old story you'd prefer to pretend is really a myth. Then later came the movie, done by one of your leading filmmakers, no less. Unfortunately, I think more people picketed the movie than actually went and saw it.

We waited a while before trying this again. Recently we came out with movies turning Noah into the crazed daddy from *The Shining*, followed by "reimagining" (one of my favorite horse pucky terms) the stutterer as a barbaric schizophrenic. With our deadbeat dad depicted as a petulant child just for good measure. Except this time we did it up right with dazzling special effects, and even got your feckless media to promote it. But alas, those movies flopped as well. Turns out no matter how lost your culture is, you still want your heroes to actually be something you can look up to.

So if we couldn't corrupt your heroes, that meant we had to corrupt you.

We had to corrupt you to the point that you could no longer contemplate aspiring to be like your heroes. So altruistic. So pure. So brave. We had to corrupt you to the point that you would begin changing your heroes for us, in order to make them more "relatable" and "contemporary."

We had to convince you that on one hand you're just fine the way you are and human nature is basically good, but on the other hand convince you that attempting to rise above your base nature was arrogant and judgmental.

At first blush, these would seem to be contradictory notions and thus an impossible task. But that's why I get paid the big bucks.

I found the answer in a new twist on an old tactic—decadence.

When people think decadence, they think of someone like our beloved Nero (who is one of the better-treated troglodytes down here) "marrying" his male slave inside the Roman Senate. Or mass pagan orgies to "gods" of the harvest (see that as us in disguise). It's doubtful your culture will ever go for such overt public decadence, because even now there's sadly still a strong element of those within your borders who wish to follow "you know who."

Typically, we would consider such a remnant to be a threat, for your history proves it does not take a majority to prevail. Let's be honest here—we usually have the numbers. However, a persistent minority armed with unwavering courage of conviction, or just one such person even, is usually our most formidable foe. Yet right now we pay it no mind, because you're not listening to the remnant remaining in your culture. You're shunning them, siding with us, and helping us to permanently silence them.

Because, "tolerance." All thanks to the new type of decadence I contrived.

A decadence based on dysfunction.

What if we took the legalism, hypocrisy, and judgmental streak that moralistic cultures are stereotypically known for, and swung the pendulum so far the other way that having any moral standard at all made you out to be a "bigot" or a "hater"?

Except we'd need a force powerful enough to be capable of destabilizing the cultural influence of your churches; otherwise we couldn't replace moral clarity with moral confusion no matter how compelling our propaganda.

More problematic is the fact "you know who" made his natural law an often self-enforcing mechanism. Meaning there are commonsense rewards for doing what he says is right, and commonsense consequences for doing what he claims is wrong. Even in your most debauched state you tend to respond to these commonsense stimuli more often than not, so we'd also need a force powerful enough to incentivize you to ignore the reality written into your DNA.

When I posed this hypothesis to my fellow demon generals, their snarky corporate response was akin to your dismissive "good luck with that." They thought no such force on earth existed, and it would take decades of trial and error for us to manufacture it. They claimed my plan wasn't viable.

Little did they know I had already identified a force capable of wreaking such havoc. Even better, this was a force ordained by none other than our deadbeat dad himself. Talk about hoisting him on his own petard.

That force is government.

I remember the day I first laid out what I'm about to share with you to my Master in front of my peers. I took a big risk with this one, and would've certainly been punished (for my own good, of course) had it proven to be a harebrained scheme and a waste of my Master's precious time.

On second thought, though, it shouldn't have seemed so far-fetched if you stop and think about it. Most governments throughout your miserable existence have claimed to be the ultimate authority on this planet (but always remember this is my Master's world). Caesars have claimed to be gods. Kings have claimed a divine right to rule. Marxist governments claim there isn't a god, therefore the highest authority is the government itself. And so on and so forth.

Therefore, is it really such a stretch to push government in this direction, since it really wants to go there anyway?

Still, the way your government was constructed wasn't going to make this easy. After all, governments tend to turn on their people when they're defenseless, not when they're armed to the teeth like you people are.

I admit I was stymied by that one for a bit. Okay, like maybe for ten minutes or something, until I figured out the way to get around an armed citizenry is not to have the government turn on a people that can shoot back. Instead, we'll get the people to *need* the government, and then you'll voluntarily beat your swords into plowshares for us.

Unfortunately, that begged another question. How were we going to get the most prosperous people in history, who established the first viable middle class in history, to need their government that much? What could create such a need?

The breakdown of the family would do it, but how to go about it? It's not like we could start out with a "your family sucks" message. Although nowadays we are that brazen, and you even give awards to the movies and television shows we make based on that theme (*snort*).

Nonetheless, even you bags of meat are too smart to fall for a full frontal assault at first, which is why you never see my Master wearing a red unitard complete with a pitchfork (although I bet he'd rock it if he did). Thus, coming right out and saying "get hooked on government so we can destroy your most foundational institution" probably wouldn't sell.

But using government to "save" the family sure would.

So to "save" you, we evolved your social safety net into a full-fledged welfare state. For a safety net implies a temporary rescue when you're overwhelmed, not a permanent state of being—which is exactly what a welfare state is.

We needed you to feel permanently entitled to government, which is really saying you're entitled to steal from your neighbor because he may have more of something than you do. That's not "fair" don't you know.

That's right, dear troglodytes, we (really I) took the sin of covetousness and made it its own political constituency thanks to the welfare state. Come on, you can say it. No, really, go right ahead.

You're right. I'm a genius.

Some of you who call yourselves people of that dreadful book will beg to differ with me here. Claiming that what I'm describing is really "charity." Please explain to me how charity can be compulsory, you moron. Good grief, does this demon even have to teach you theology, too?

Doesn't that dreadful book say "you know who" loves a "cheerful giver"? Are even your bleeding heart liberals cheerful when they file their taxes? Wasn't one of those genuflecting statists on cable news recently busted for owing more in unpaid taxes than 75 percent of Americans make in a year? Do you know of anyone who volunteers to pay even more taxes than what they're required in the name of charity?

Of course not. I'm not sure what's sillier, your species or the arguments it devises and devours hook, line, and sinker sometimes.

Since it's obvious I'm more familiar with the teachings of that dreadful book than many of you are (and why that's the case will be explained later on), allow me to let you in on a little secret. The point of charity is to demonstrate the love of "you know who" to those who don't know him as intimately as true believers do.

Sitting back and watching Auntie Sam confiscate a good portion of your earnings before you even see them isn't charity. It's just confiscation—which is stealing, plain and simple. There's no connection made there between creator and created. There's just a financial transaction from the person who made it to the person who didn't, and therefore has no legitimate claim on it.

Otherwise known as a scam. Take it from me. This whole thing was my idea. I'm a lying minion who works for the Father of Lies, remember?

When that government check comes in the mail to the disadvantaged, who is given the gratitude and the glory for it? Is it "you know who"? No, it's your government. The same government, by the way, currently eradicating him from public life. It is now government by which you live and breathe. Once government becomes the source of your provision, it will eventually become the source of your everything else as well (morality, education, law, etc.).

Even here in Hell, the truth is whoever cuts the check is the one calling the shots.

The welfare state operates under the premise that the reason people make bad choices isn't because your species has fallen from grace and is in need of redemption, but that people just lack the resources needed to be "equal" with those making good choices. So we take from the people who took advantage of their opportunity to make it, which undermines the meritocracy that made you the envy of the world, and give it to the people who have yet to.

This kills two birds with one stone.

First, it creates class division. Justice is no longer blind and "the man" is keeping you down, giving you a convenient excuse for all the stupid stuff you do that keeps you from making it. You then break down into a tribal survival of the fittest, with government (also made up of flawed human beings, but you often overlook that) playing referee among the masses.

This also creates a capricious society where the rule of law no longer applies, because the rules can always be changed by the next election based on whose passions are the most enflamed at the time. This uncertain dynamic keeps stoking the flames of discontent. Now you're no longer a melting pot of disparate peoples forging into one, but a culture awash in chaos.

And never forget, we are agents of chaos.

Second, it also convinces the people on the receiving end of the welfare state that they're just fine the way they are. There's no need for them to take responsibility for their own lives and attempt to reach their divinely given potential. As a result, they're essentially caught in no man's land. Too poor to truly be independent and free, too well off to want to. For example, a recent story out of Pennsylvania found a single mother could "earn" over

$80,000 per year in various welfare state benefits. Now instead of passing on your "American Dream," you're passing down cycles and generations of dependency.

Of course, not everyone who stumbles in life does so from a self-inflicted wound. Sometimes bad things do happen to good people, which are some of my most joyous occasions. Sometimes the rich and powerful prey upon the poor and helpless. Sometimes the corporation preys upon its employees. Sometimes races and ethnicities prey upon one another. But this again is a result of the fact you're rotten at the core. That whole "original sin" thing we've convinced you is religious myth, but is as true as true can be.

By doing so, we were then able to convince you that pretty much everybody in an inferior position in the culture is automatically a—say it with me now—"victim!"

The introduction of victimology into your culture was the Rosetta Stone that unlocked the rest of what you'll read in this book, and it's also the primary reason you're doomed. No one is accountable for their actions anymore. Everyone has an excuse. And if you don't accept the victimhood, then you're guilty of an offense worse than the one committed by the offender.

You're a hater.

Originally, it was just those of a more liberal persuasion who bought into this, with women and minorities perpetual targets of some sinister yet unseen institutional "white male privilege" that gave everybody a Get Out of Jail Free card for their lot in life.

Listen, I know what real white male privilege looks and feels like. I and some of my brethren literally possessed the bodies of those racists who doused blacks with high-pressure water hoses back in the day. I've lynched a few in my time as well. Now *that* is some real white male privilege for sure. You don't know what white male privilege truly is nowadays. You're so stupid that even after electing a black man to be president, who attended a racist church that took its words right from our script, you're still suffering from "white liberal guilt."

This brings me to a quick sidebar.

You want to break the heart of your creator? Then do these three things (in no particular order):

Become an anti-Semite.

Devalue and oppress a fellow human being because you deem them lower than you based on race, creed, color, economic status, etc.

Massacre your own children.

You will grieve the most powerful being in the universe if you do these three things, because his most important commandments are to love him with everything you have, and then to love your neighbor as you love yourself. You can't obey those commandments if you commit acts that so blatantly go against his nature such as these.

But I digress.

Since I and all of Hell could give a rip about obeying him, we do these things in abundance—whenever and wherever we can. "If it feels good, do it" we always say, and doing these things never feels better then when you're doing them with (or for) us.

Of course, you bags of meat will look to get over on each other any chance you'll get. That's the human condition. But that's a far cry from some institutional racism/xenophobia/sexism the victimology we planted in your elite cultural enclaves claims you have. You'd think this victimology thing would've jumped the shark when you saw private property, owned by blacks, being looted by black rioters to protest racism in the recent Ferguson riots—but stupid is as stupid does, I suppose.

I think I did my job a little too good. Case in point: Ask one of your perpetually offended when America will finally be freed of its inequality. They can't give you an answer. Why? Because they can't imagine an America when that would ever be true. They're literally hard-wired for victim status, thus a culture that doesn't default to victimology would be as foreign to them as a World Series would be to a Chicago Cubs fan. (That might be my cheapest shot yet.)

Don't like the fact that the fewest Americans are working since the 1970s? You're just a racist who hates a black president. Don't like the fact you're paying for the college tuition of illegal aliens? You're just a hater. Think kids are best off being raised by a married mom and dad? You're a bigot.

I love this stuff!

But wait, it gets better.

There's an old saying: "Treason never prospers. What's the reason? Because whenever treason prospers, none dare call it treason."

Turns out what's good for the goose is good for the gander. So now the guys on the right are playing the victim card with regularity, too.

Like if you made some really stupid business decisions, you don't go belly-up anymore. Nowadays you're "too big to fail" and your cronies in Congress bail you out. How about if your religious movie fails to gain a following? It's not because your movie sucks, complete with the ultra-cheesy conversion scene that even other believers think is the cinematic equivalent to fingernails on a chalkboard. Oh no, it's because Hollywood hates conservative Christians, that's why.

Which is true, by the way, but your movie still sucks.

Better yet, "the devil made me do it" has now become "the devil did this to me." Like the devil got me fired from my job. No, idiot, you were late three days in a row. That's why you were fired from your job. Get a freaking alarm clock.

Apparently my Master is so brilliant he's now getting credit for the work he didn't even do!

All of this excuse making also has a boomerang effect. Since everybody's a victim, that also means nobody is. People grow so tired of hearing the excuses they have no patience for true injustice now. When someone is legitimately discriminated against, you sigh because it's the boy who cried wolf.

Chaos! Chaos! Chaos!

We are now well into your second generation of this welfare state dysfunction, and the decadence is on the rise. Nearly every household, regardless of social status, is now tainted by the sexual revolution that immediately followed the implementation of the welfare state.

By the way, that is not a "chicken or the egg" argument. We had to have the welfare state in place *before* we introduced the new moral order, because if there wasn't a welfare state already in place people would still have to pay the consequences for their immoral actions themselves.

Then the decadence would've been relegated to the elite classes that could've afforded it, as we've seen in previous eras. Poor and middle class folks can't afford recreational sex with multiple partners well into their thirties, mistresses on the side, and baby daddies on their own. They need marriage not just for love, but that commitment to also stabilize them financially. This explains why one of the likeliest ways to lower a mother and her children's standing of living is via divorce.

The welfare state became the condom of the sexual revolution. It implied "protection" from the consequences of opening Pandora's box, without considering the unintended consequences. Sure, a condom is a reliable way to avoid an unplanned pregnancy, but it doesn't protect you from the baggage that comes from bringing your sexual experiences with other partners with you into your marriage, and the conflicts that creates. It also doesn't avoid the heartbreak that comes from giving the most intimate aspects of yourselves to each other without any real commitment in exchange.

Similarly, the welfare state means never having to say you're sorry for your immorality. But it doesn't mean you avoid all the newly discovered STDs, the divorce culture, the pornography gluttony, and family dysfunction that largely didn't exist in your culture until the last fifty years.

But since we gave you what your wicked little hearts really wanted deep down all along—pleasure *and* irresponsibility—you never really stopped to think about that ahead of time, did you? Thanks again for being what you are.

I'd almost feel sorry for you if I were capable of empathy. Okay, that's a lie, but I almost had you for a minute.

Unfortunately for all of you reading this, the dysfunction is so widespread in your culture now that the decadence is abundant. For evil's sake, I've seen studies that show a healthy segment of your own pastors are currently struggling with chronic masturbation. There are so many sheep without a shepherd. Needless to say, down here we are downright giddy about that.

See, with every household now tainted by the decadence, there is no longer a standard to be held accountable to. For anybody that attempts to hold someone else to a standard higher than your base desires is automatically a hypocrite, because at some point they would've partaken in the decadence, too. And the absolute lowest form of knuckle dragger to be nowadays is a hypocrite.

Of course, you could easily combat that argument with humility, transparency, and accountability. In other words, admit that you have also sinned against "you know who," ask him for forgiveness and the strength to overcome your weakness, and open yourself up to accountability to do right going forward. Then admit when/if you do stumble in the future and get right back up again.

But I think we both know you won't do that. You're proud of your dysfunction, and you should be. You're good enough. You're smart enough. And doggone it, people like you. You own your decadence. No one is the boss of you. Anybody that doesn't affirm what you desire is a racist/hater/bigot. A judgmental hypocrite who's condemning you for doing what they're probably doing as well. I say screw them, and so do you.

Society shouldn't just affirm your desires. It should also subsidize them! You're the victim here, remember?

There, that's it. You're nodding your head in agreement with me. Contemplating whether to stop reading for now because you're feeling that familiar twitch in your loins to go and check out the Internet's fleshy spoils once again.

Go ahead, your wife and kids are asleep. You're not hurting anybody. We're all consenting adults here, right? Well, except for the girls kidnapped into the sex trafficking trade who are forced into televised prostitution, but that's not important now. It's all about you, and your desires. That's what's important here and always.

Besides, isn't she always nagging you with those "honey do" lists as it is? And doesn't she go to bed without you most nights with her sweatpants on, which might as well be an "all lanes are closed" sign? You deserve this.

You've got nothing to lose. I mean, it's not like your teenager daughter could walk in on you or anything, colossally embarrassing you and scarring her psyche for life. And it's not like your son might discover what his dad is doing late at night, pick up your nasty habit, and then take it with him into his own family in the future. Set those thoughts aside, and do what you do best—put you first.

In case you need to be reminded of some of your favorite haunts, I'll subtly suggest them to you now. I'm the still, small voice in your head that sounds like you, remember, and tells you what you want to hear at times like these. Never forget who's got your back and never judges you.

All right then, carry on. This is your show. I'll still be here when you get back. Hell, we might even tune in.

CHAPTER 4

Debt

Have you looked at your balance sheet lately? I'm asking for a friend.

Seriously, the numbers are truly staggering if you itemize them. But in short they say this: you're totally and irrevocably screwed.

You are officially the worst debtor nation in the undistinguished history of this wretched world. Congratulations on your self-imposed slavery! Take a bow. Better yet, on your knees. You might as well start practicing now.

Allow me to share the actual numbers with you, if only because it will be yet another worthwhile reminder of how truly awesome I am, and how truly toast you are.

At the time I was writing this, your national debt was $18 trillion. To put that astronomical number in perspective, if you spent just $1 per day every day since the carpenter was born more than two thousand years ago, you wouldn't have spent $1 trillion by now, let alone eighteen. In fact, you'd still be $300 billion short of that.

If your national debt were laid out in a single file line of $1 bills, it would stretch from your planet all the way past Uranus. Obviously, there's a joke there, and the joke is on you. By the way, the planet Uranus is almost two billion miles away. Good thing for us there's plenty of your anuses running your government right here at home.

Your debt is 103 percent of your gross domestic product (I won't explain to you what GDP means because we made you too stupid to figure that out), and 540 percent of your annual federal revenues. This means the most valuable asset in your economy—by far, with no close second—is your debt! Every American household on average is on the hook for $148,000 of that, and only about 5 percent of American households make that much money annually as it is.

This doesn't even count the over $128 trillion in unfunded mandates and liabilities your government will need to fully fund the welfare state and your so-called "entitlements" (Social Security, Medicare, and Medicaid). That's $34 trillion more than the total net worth of your country.

To put that number in perspective, there isn't another nation on earth whose total net worth is as high as your current cash flow deficit.

Every household in America would need to pay an *additional* $580,000 to cover that shortfall, and only 1 percent of American households bring home that kind of bacon.

By 2025, the interest alone on all your debt will balloon to $785 billion. That is roughly the cost of your entire Social Security program at the moment.

If the interest you owe on your debt were its own economy, it would be the twenty-eighth richest nation in the world. Richer than the Philippines, South Africa, Iraq, Belgium, Switzerland, and Sweden—just to name a few.

And you show no signs of slowing your roll. In the past six years you've accumulated $7.5 trillion in debt, which is as much debt as you accumulated combined in your first 228 years of existence. There are currently more Americans on food stamps then the total population of Spain.

As if all that dread weren't enough, I haven't even shared with you my absolutely favorite stat yet.

Communist China, the only nation on earth that comes close to being able to challenge you economically and militarily, owns $1.3 trillion of your foreign debt. Because nothing says "stupid" like making your adversary your landlord.

Hey, while you're at it, stop by the gas station and fill her up again. All those who wish to conquer you in the name of Allah thank you! And so do I!

It turns out the decadence we offered you, that you now enjoy, came with a price tag after all. Santa charged his goodie bag to your credit card. You should've listened to your elders and those crusty old conservatives when they warned you "there's no such thing as a free lunch."

But once you fully embraced the decadence of your new normal, and many of your bad decisions became incentivized thus freeing you from their immediate consequences, someone still had to pay for the collateral damage of violating the natural laws of "you know who." You may naively think your "entitlements" are free, but the meter's been running this entire time (with compounding interest).

There are currently 148 million Americans collecting entitlement checks of some sort from the US taxpayer, but there are only 86 million taxpayers working in the private sector paying into the system. Government workers are at best a revenue-neutral transaction—they pay taxes, but taxes from the private sector pay for their jobs. That means there are 70 percent more tax takers than taxpayers.

The outlook here continues to be bleak. Right now almost 93 million Americans are out of work. That is a staggering number. To hammer home to you just how staggering, consider that if your unemployed were their own country they would be the fifteenth most populous nation on earth. Bigger than Egypt, France, Italy, and even the United Kingdom.

Wait a second, it just dawned on me you probably don't know much of anything at all about those "natural laws" I just referenced, do you? Of course you don't, because we made sure to remove all that information from your schools. More on that later.

In the meantime, that means almost all of you reading this really have no idea whatsoever how this planet works. You're literally the blind leading the blind. This also means you really aren't fully aware of what we've done to you. And if you aren't fully aware of what we've done to you, then that steals at least some of my joy watching you circle the drain.

I suppose since your fate is sealed I can go ahead and let you in on what the generations who founded and built your country understood and submitted to, but which you're either ignorant of or hostile to. It's just too much fun to pass on revealing to you one of the basic fundamentals of your existence that would've preserved your freedom if only you had heard and obeyed.

See, our deadbeat dad cares enough about you to tell you "no" the same way an earthly parent tells a child not to play in traffic, touch a hot stove, or stick his tongue in the electrical outlet. When your progenitors chose the ways of my Master long ago, and disobeyed our deadbeat dad in the process, they cursed all of their future offspring with a defiant spirit. As a result, it is not natural for you to do what our deadbeat dad says is right. Instead, you often crave what he says is wrong. You'll even kill each other for it.

Would you like to know what it looks like when nobody tells you no? Then look no further than Detroit.

Flashback to the 1950s, when Detroit was the wealthiest city in America. But that is before it decided it could say yes to everything, and nobody and nothing was worthy of saying no to.

Now the city owes over 100,000 creditors and has filed for bankruptcy. It's home to over seventy hazardous waste dumps. Its population is the lowest it's been since before Henry Ford invented the assembly line. It lost 25 percent of its population in the last census alone. It has over 78,000 abandoned homes, which is more abandoned homes than the second-largest city in Montana has people.

Almost half the city's residents are illiterate. Roughly 60 percent of the city's children live in poverty. The violent crime rate is five times the national average. Only 7 percent of the city's eighth graders are reading proficient. The city has less than 10 percent of the manufacturing jobs it had fifty years ago. One of every three pregnancies ends with a mom killing her unborn child.

Thanks to your belief in your basic goodness, which comes right from my Master's encouragement that you can be like "you know who" if you just follow your own instincts and not his instructions, you have become the worst evil ever unleashed upon the creation. Detroit is living proof of this.

Honestly (and as a demon I don't use that word often), your capacity for evil rivals even our own. That's a compliment by the way. Seriously, there are times when your species takes our wicked hints/suggestions and carries them to lengths not even I—the elite demon general in all of Hell—have contrived yet.

Pro tip: it's not really "the devil made me do it" as much as it's "the devil *helped* me do it," because you really wanted to do it all along. We can't "make" you do anything. We can't even materialize a temporal form on our own, which is why at times we've had to possess yours. We're more like the frosting to your cake. We're merely the additive, not the recipe.

Even if we weren't here at all, you'd still be damned all on your own. You already started the fire. We just add lighter fluid. Or, as we like to say down here, "more cowbell."

But the sentimental sap known as your creator isn't content to leave well enough alone. So just as he sent the carpenter to take the punishment all of you reading this so richly deserve upon himself, he established basic parameters of justice within the creation itself to incentivize right behavior and discourage our (your) preferred behavior.

These parameters have been known by different names down through the ages, but in your nation's history they became known as "the Laws of Nature and of Nature's g-d." Often referred to as "natural law" for short, it basically means heaven's honor code. Despite all your scornful mocking and disobedience, our deadbeat dad still doesn't want you to destroy yourselves. So he ordained this "natural law" as a system of good consequences for doing what's good for you, and bad consequences for doing what's bad for you.

Take all your red ink I just laid out as an example. That's there because you keep trying to use government to do the things the natural law doesn't permit it to do. "You know who" established four spheres of authority to maintain order in your fallen world: self, family, church, and state (government). Each of them has their own distinct jurisdictions, but are simultaneously under the authority of the natural law. Whenever you bags of meat try to move these spheres out of their divinely ordained jurisdictions, tyranny happens. And there are few greater tyrannies for a people than debt.

Repeatedly you are asking the state (government) to operate in the spheres that traditionally belonged to the family (government acting as a surrogate father or husband) and/or the church (government acting as an agent of compassion and charity). "You know who" intended the state's primary jurisdiction to be the promotion of good by punishing evil. The state is to be the instrument of justice against all enemies of the natural law, both foreign (invading armies) and domestic (transgressors against the natural law, or "criminals").

These repeated violations of the natural law are the reason for all this debt you currently have. Did you know that only 29 percent of your budget is what's called "discretionary spending"? The budget for your military, which is government's most basic necessity according to the natural law, is 55 percent of that.

That sounds like a lot, until you realize the other two-thirds of your budget is called "mandatory spending" and about 90 percent of that is your welfare state entitlement spending. By 2024, should you last that long (and I have my doubts), that welfare state entitlement spending is projected to be 85 percent of your spending growth. So even if you eliminated your entire military altogether, you'd barely put a dent in your debt.

Your attempts to impose "charity" (which by definition is voluntary and therefore cannot be imposed) via the secular state instead of the family and the church are literally killing you. It can't possibly work, because our dear old dad wants his creatures to know where mercy and charity truly come from—his love for you and your love for one another. He will not allow any government, especially one following our lead in erasing his name and word from public view, to prosper against the divine plan. The more you foolishly try, the more in debt you become.

However, thanks to our propaganda as well as your own selfish desires, you don't see it that way. You see his natural laws as a hindrance to your self-actualization, not as a hedge of protection. With a subtle nudge from us, you have broken free of the shackles of his divine blessing and guidance, and become our ball and chain instead.

Case in point: Several years ago there was a judge from down south somewhere . . . I forget the place . . . no, it wasn't Texas, although I hate that place. That's right, it was Alabama. He simply wanted to post the "ten commandments" at his courthouse, just as they've been displayed in the US Supreme Court building all along. And were also originally omnipresent in every public building from coast to coast in your history.

Of course, we got our people on it right away. Lawsuits were filed, threats were made—by now you know the drill. Yet he was unlike most of your effeminate bureaucrats you call public officials. He actually called our bluff and dared to say the emperor has no clothes. That our people really didn't have any power to do anything about it (which is true, but that's not important now), and were all hat and no cattle.

Thankfully, my Master was "vacationing" in Pyongyang while this was transpiring, because I will confess that's the last time I thought there was any chance at all our plan would fail. And as you know, my Master doesn't take too kindly to even potential failure.

Understand that if this one Alabama judge were allowed to call our bluff and our hand was revealed to be deuce/seven off suit and not pocket aces, it would encourage an entire movement of like-minded men and women to finally find their courage after all these years. Without the courts, most of our greatest schemes are up in smoke. Fear and intimidation are our biggest weapons. Therefore, we had to maintain the pernicious lie that once some unelected judge(s) has spoken, that's now the law of the land. No matter how lawless it is.

Frankly, it's the tactical linchpin to the whole plan. It's always easier and more effective for us to infiltrate the elite classes and have them be the ones who impose chaos on the masses from on high. It's when the masses take control of their own fate, just as your founding fathers did, that we're on the defensive. Does not that dreadful book say something about "when the righteous rule the people rejoice" and "a triple-braided chord is tougher to break"?

I'm getting a lump in my chest just remembering those nerve-wracking days. Even when he's on sabbatical, my Master likes to stay informed. So I was still to report to him daily about how the plan to take you down was proceeding. Had he known then of this threat, who knows how severely I would've been punished. Disembowelment might have been lenient. That's why I had to lie to him: "see no good, hear no good" is what I reported to him each day.

Right about now you're probably wondering why I would openly admit in print that I lied to my Master, and am I not afraid of retribution for doing so? Remember, my Master had to approve this manuscript before you read it, so he already knows that I lied to him. However, since I lied to him and used that to buy myself the time it took to devise a way to keep the plan on track, I received a commendation for "original thinking" from my Master!

Nevertheless, at the time I ain't too proud to admit I was scrambling. We threw everything but the kitchen sink at this Alabama judge, and he wasn't wavering. His boldness was starting to become a national story now, and many folks in your ranks who had embraced defeatism were starting to get inspired. There was even talk of your "conservative movement" lining up behind this judge, and urging the president of the United States from the same political party to stand with him and use this as a galvanizing moment for "patriots" across the nation.

THAT ABSOLUTELY COULD NOT HAPPEN!

Thankfully, we had one or two key people on the inside that convinced a few others if the precedent of this judge standing up to our big lie was allowed to stand, then you folks were going to demand similar boldness from the rest of your governing class in the future once this example was set. And that boldness could come with a steep price, including the loss of their major fundraising streams and even their elected offices.

If there's one constant in the universe, it's the fecklessness of a politician. "Better for one man to die than for our whole nation [see that as *scam*] to perish" is still one of my favorite lines in that dusty bible most of you rarely read.

Thus, I played our tried-and-true trump card once more, and it came up aces. Even some of the judge's fellow "Christian conservative" legal beagles openly turned on him, and they kneecapped him for us in broad daylight—Luca Brasi style. All to preserve their lives of luxury and nonconfrontation. In the name of Jee-zus, of course.

Damn. I mean, *damn*.

I need a cigarette after witnessing your species' depravity like that. It's moments like those that almost make me regret having to torment your species for eternity once you arrive down here. Note that I said "almost."

Don't get me wrong—as I wrote before, we demons get off on your bloodcurdling screams and pleas for mercy when none is forthcoming. But truly there are some among your species that could even teach a demon a thing or two about treachery. Sometimes even we demons of Hell have to give you bags of meat your props, as your kids say today.

I'll tell you what; I'm not totally devoid of compassion. So if any of those tremendously clutch traitors decides not to repent between now and when they assume room temperature, I'll petition my Master to permit them the eternal equivalent of one of your days for forbearance of torment.

Of course, we're a stickler for rules down here, so if that forbearance is granted that means double the torment the next day to make up for it. But it's the least I can do since several of those modern-day Caiaphases literally saved my scaly bacon.

There, never let it be said I've never performed a good deed in my life. Now get off my lawn!

Once this potential insurgency was put down, by people supposedly on your own side no less, there was literally no line of defense remaining between you and us. Sure, you have some of your politicians and bloggers urging that stance be taken again, and that same Alabama judge is even back in power as well. But while any attempt at righteousness no matter how trivial annoys us, these efforts at restoring the natural law of "you know who" into a place of prominence within your society are little more than pesky gnats.

They're going to go nowhere because you're too far gone now, which is why I have no qualms at all about openly discussing all of this. Even many of you reading this that have the right worldview falsely believe you can only fight to the extent public opinion allows, instead of boldly working to mold, shape, and change public opinion. You may still cling to all that high-and-mighty "g-d talk" but you don't really mean it.

Rather than risk his wrath by obeying him instead of us, you will bow the knee to Baal at the altar of (manipulated) public opinion just the same. Better yet, you'll completely bastardize a few verses from that dreadful book and club your own would-be heroes of history over the head with them. Hell, nowadays you're practically better at crushing your team morale than we are.

I mean you wouldn't want to be one of those "radicals," would you? Funny thing is, those discredited radicals are always the ones that change history. (John the Baptist, anyone?) Thankfully, you're too driven by your own comfort to remember that.

Case in point: The past few years we have intercepted many promising (for us) conversations among the generations of older men in positions of leadership. In past eras, these aging movers and shakers would be concerned about their legacy, and at this stage of their lives looking to actively groom the leaders who would pick up their mantle.

Except all too often they are not.

Many of your churches have no heir apparent waiting in the wings, and then slowly wither away and die once the lead pastor(s) retire or assume room temperature. In your political circles we have repeatedly seen the older, more complacent men look to stifle and shun their younger, more aggressive peers. They even chastise the younger men for being "obstructionist" or "out of the mainstream." All because they seek to confront and defeat our schemes rather than placate or regulate them.

Do the brash younger men need training, honing, and disciplining to fulfill their calling? Absolutely. And the older generation of men could provide that. Yet they not only frequently pass on doing so, but they go even further by trying to snuff out the spark/passion/purpose the younger men were divinely given for "such a time as this."

Who knows why. Perhaps it's because they see the younger men's warrior spirit as an indictment of their generational failure, and they don't want to be reminded of such. Perhaps it's something else entirely. Regardless of the motivation, the results are the same—you have a tendency to take out our potential threats before we have to.

That's why we don't have anything to worry about. Let's face it, most of you aren't even going to bother reading the rest of this book, believing it's way too over the top at this point to be true. So you'll pick up the remote and seek out a little "reality" instead, like *Sister Wives*.

Because nothing says "reality" like a total goofball getting multiple women to do his bidding for him in the laundry and kitchen on national television, all the while he takes turns with them in the bedroom. Yeah, sure, that happens in real life. You might as well watch another paternity test marathon of *Maury Povich Show* reruns while you're at it.

You may doubt that what I am telling you is real, but the consequences for your doubt and disobedience of his natural laws are very, very real.

All the goodies promised to you from your government are not free. That's why you're so in debt. All the guiltless pleasures we tempt you with are not free, either. For example, much of the porn most "consenting adults" consume came at the high price of human trafficking.

But there's no need for you to worry about all that right now. For now just sit back, relax, and enjoy the show. You don't have to worry about paying back that debt until you get down here, but you should know that down here paybacks are a female dog—and she has a nasty bite.

For some of you reading this, that's still a long ways off. For others it could be as soon as tomorrow. But one thing is for certain in Hell—you can check in any time you like, but you can never leave.

CHAPTER 5

Dunces

Among my recent favorites of your movies is one very few of you actually saw, which means you missed out on a chance to preview your very near future.

The movie is called *Idiocracy*. It's a (self) parody of what happens to a culture that has been dumbed down to become a mindless herd of low-information voting, sex-obsessed miscreants and lazy bums. You know, like your culture is currently becoming. Unintentional self-fulfilling prophecy is always the best!

You are way down this road to perdition now, and it's too late to turn back. But had you listened to your founding fathers and not to us, it would not have been so.

See, they established two defense perimeters—the church and the schools—to prevent someone like, well, me from taking you down from within. While we're always hard at work on your churches, and have turned a good many of them into little more than do-gooder money changers, that's still a long, hard road.

The carpenter is particularly problematic when it comes to sticking his nose into our business where your churches are concerned. He has a tendency to fight for your churches the way a devoted husband fights for his wife. The carpenter is quite ferocious when he wants to be, and nothing like the harmless hippy shaman of antiquity we've sold him to you as.

He's also just a little bit possessive about the church, which explains why we've never been successful at completely overturning that corporate institution. Even during the Dark Ages, or whenever a culture goes morally dark like you're about to, there's usually at least a remnant of the self-righteous remaining to pester us right to the bitter end. Thus, we've adjusted our goals where churches are concerned. As we say here in Hell: if at first you don't succeed, lower your standards.

So our expectation for your churches is simply to turn enough of them our way to get them fighting among one another, and/or to make sure we've got at least some people who look and speak like church folk representing us and our message to the culture at large. And hot damn, don't we have a whole battalion of such folks at the moment. Especially in your seminaries, ironically enough. Turns out the longer you stay there pondering the lint in your navel, *the less likely* you are to believe the words of that dreadful book.

These quislings are lining up for us now, looking to make their "mark" for my Master (pardon the eschatological pun there).

The beautiful thing is we don't even have to pay them anymore because you're paying them for us. The amount of money you send these hair gel–infested proxies of Hell in the hopes of a "blessing" is breathtaking. For example, one of our phony "faith healers" lives in Beverly Hills. He recently had a heart attack after returning home from a "missions" trip, which really means fleecing a bunch of turd-world primates that can't read or write. All in the name of Jee-zus. The funny thing is his family was worried about the news getting out there about his condition, because it prompts an obvious question:

"How come the faith healer can't heal himself?"

We're not worried about that, though. This particular guy has already been discredited many times, but you keep "sowing a seed" into his (our) pockets nonetheless. Besides, even if this particular cat has exhausted his nine lives, we'll just raise up another even more ridiculous than he was. You will buy it, because you want to believe literally *anything* other than the truth.

Most of these pinheads we recruit, train, and deploy couldn't get a job as a Wal-Mart greeter in the real world. But if we teach them how to take a few verses about "health and wealth" completely out of context, and give them the right image (and I have no idea why you seem to be attracted to those dudes in the Hawaiian shirts who wear socks with sandals), you'll send them the money you wouldn't bother saving for your kids' college fund.

But back to the plan.

Like I said, a war of attrition within your churches, or just enough converts to our side to allow us to use your insipid news media as a platform for our propaganda, was about the best we could hope for in your culture. Unlike your European cousins, you have a system of government predicated on g-d–given rights. Therefore, we're not sure a systemic spread of secularism is possible in your country like we accomplished over there. We have calculated that there would always be a strong religious subculture here to some degree. Some remnant that will always be willing to push back against us.

That meant we had to ruthlessly target the other defense mechanism—the schools—in order to nullify the church's influence.

Read the words of your founding fathers and you'll learn all you to need to know about why your schools were our prime directive:

"Educate and inform the whole mass of the people, for they are the only sure reliance for the preservation of liberty." (Thomas Jefferson)

"The best means of forming a manly, virtuous, and happy people will be found in the right education of the youth. Without this foundation, every other means, in my opinion, will fail." (George Washington)

"Learned Institutions ought to be the favorite objects with every free people. They throw that light over the public mind, which is the best security against crafty and dangerous encroachments on the public liberty." (James Madison)

In short, your founding fathers actually wanted to have an educated and well-informed populace. Frankly, we had never heard of such a thing from a human government. Prior to your founding, whenever a human government talked about educating people it either meant one of two things: teaching the aristocracy only, or the masses would be educated to be compliant with the state.

But educating the people to protect them from even their own government if need be? That is a level of critical thinking we didn't think you were capable of.

Critical thinking is like a virus to demonic influence. In some ways we loathe it even more than the gospel itself, because our résumé has proven we can hijack even the carpenter's message if the culture receiving it doesn't encourage critical thinking.

Consider that for every martyr whose blood was shed by a despot, the carpenter's professed followers have also done so to one another by the bushel. Almost always because the peoples involved were not taught to critically think through his teachings. They followed their passions instead of his purpose. Passions that were enflamed by us.

Look at all the examples of Christian anti-Semitism throughout history. Now, let's just stop and think about how asinine that is for a second. Wasn't the carpenter Jewish? Don't his followers go to church on Sunday and worship a g-d who became a man, and that man was a Jew? So how dumb do you have to be to believe you're worshipping the carpenter by persecuting his native tribe? I mean, would you show your friend how much you love him by slapping his family around while he was away? Yes, you're this special kind of stupid without critical thinking.

Allow me to bottom line it for you. There has *never* been a successful demonic initiative into your world that didn't include the removal of critical thinking, and there *never* will be. Doesn't that dreadful book say something about his people perishing "for a lack of knowledge"? All of you bags of meat are definitely sinful and fallen, but you're definitely not all stupid.

Not by a long shot, in fact. You're still the image-bearer of the universe's only omniscient being, remember. While your puny brains don't come close to matching his in capacity, you're still much smarter than the average bear—but only when you're thinking critically. With critical thinking you can give us a run for our money. Without critical thinking you're Joe Biden on *Jeopardy*. A laugh a minute.

In that scenario, you are the antelope (prey) and we are the lion (predator). Sometimes we like to play with our food before we eat it, but rest assured eventually you will be devoured just the same.

Critical thinkers are a serious threat to us in any culture, but what if we faced an entire culture consisting of critical thinkers by and large? Why, that could even be a global threat to us, which is what you once were.

Until I came along, that is.

Ironically, I have one of your great reformers to thank for inspiring me for this portion of the plan. Martin Luther, he of the *Ninety-Five Theses* we've done our best to forbid you to read, once said this about education: "I am afraid that the schools will prove the very gates of Hell, unless they diligently labor in explaining the Holy Scriptures and engraving them in the heart of the youth."

Voila!

My first priority was making sure that dreadful book had to go. To the contemporary audiences reading this, that doesn't seem so controversial because I made what Luther feared your new normal. However, back in the day that dreadful book was a fundamental component of an American child's education.

Ever heard of *The New England Primer*? No, most of you haven't, because I'm good at what I do. But for the founding generations of your country, it was their primary textbook. It included a portrait of George Washington, and a dedication that described itself as "the little bible of New England." The introduction included a brief history of the Christian faith, as well as discussion of "sin" and "salvation."

Try teaching like this in a school these days and you're a modern-day leper, but this was standard operating procedure for those that made your liberty possible. Take a look at these examples of how *The New England Primer* taught the youngest of school children to learn the alphabet back then:

A—"In *Adam's* fall we sinned all." And no, it wasn't talking about Adam Levine. This is a reference to the Adam of Adam and Eve.

B—"Heaven to find the *bible* mind."

C—"*Christ* crucified for sinners died."

D—"The *deluge* drowned the earth around." The "deluge" refers to Noah's flood.

E—"*Elijah* hid by ravens fed." Elijah was one of Israel's peskiest prophets.

J—"*Jesus* did die for thee and I."

L—"The *lion* bold, the *lamb* does hold." Since most of you don't know what that is a reference to, the carpenter is referred to as both "the lion of Judah" and "the lamb of g-d" in that dreadful book you no longer read.

N—"*Noah* did view the world old and new."

P—"*Peter* denies his Lord and cries." This is a reference to the fisherman denying his allegiance to the carpenter three times on the night we beat him senseless.

Q—"*Queen* Esther came in royal state to save the Jews from dismal fate." This is a direct reference to a beloved story in that dreadful book.

R—"*Rachel* does mourn for her fifth-born." Rachel is one of the Jewish matriarchs.

S—"*Samuel* anoints whom g-d appoints." Samuel is the judge who anoints David as king of Israel by the authority of "you know who."

U—"*Uriah's* beautiful wife made David take his life." Uriah is the husband King David had sent off to war to die so that he could steal his wife, Bathsheba.

Z—"*Zacchaeus* did climb the tree for our Lord to see." This is a story about a little dweeb so desperate to see the carpenter he risked his life for a passing glance.

Yikes! And people think we're guilty of indoctrination? Well, what do you call this? The schools established by your founding fathers sought to introduce the next generation to our dear old dad and the teachings of that dreadful book right away. The reason being is they viewed it as the antidote to our ability to poison you as we had every other great civilization in history up until that point.

And they were right—emphasis on *were*.

This encouragement of critical thinking even carried over into civic affairs. For example, at the time your Constitution was being debated for ratification by the states, a few of your founding fathers published what later became known as *The Federalist Letters*. These were a series of treatises published in newspapers throughout the original thirteen states explaining the meaning of your Constitution, and answering challenges to its provisions as well as concerns about its wording.

Today's law school students struggle to grasp the meaning of these essays, which contain some of the highest-level prose your species is capable of. However, these essays were originally written for an audience with an eighth-grade education back in the latter eighteenth century. That was typically the age young adults either finished their education and became a laborer (farmer, family trade, apprenticeship, etc.) or went on to college for more formal study (law, medicine, seminary, etc.). Many of those colleges were what you refer to today as Ivy League schools, and all of them were originally founded as seminaries or with the spreading of the carpenter's gospel as one of their main missions.

That's right, your Ivy League centers of elite secular enlightenment were originally founded as the training ground for the g-d squad. Fun fact: Harvard's original motto was "Truth for Christ and the Church." Today the motto has been shortened to just "truth" thanks to political correctness. And if you're bowing the knee to political correctness, which is really just the same prohibitions against critical thinking we've always used but we updated just for you, then unvarnished truth is most likely in short supply. Unless it's the "truth" from a certain (preapproved by yours truly) point of view.

Indulge me a moment as I brag once more.

A few paragraphs ago I referenced *The Federalist Letters*. However, there is no such thing. They were actually called *The Federalist Papers*, yet I've done such a thorough job of blinding you to your birthright you didn't even notice. Hell, I could've called them *The Penthouse Forum* and you nitwits probably wouldn't have known the difference but just nodded right along.

I'm just that good.

So what were *The Federalist Papers*, by the way? Now, please don't mistake even a modicum of respect for my opponent with reverence for the subject matter. For those are two totally different things. As someone whose only reason for being is to extend my Master's dominion, I hated all that drivel about liberty found within those words.

Nonetheless, in spite of myself I had to respect the effort those meat bags made to transparently rally their fellow primates to form "a more perfect union." That transparency is quite the contrast from what you see from your government today, which of course I deserve at least some of the credit for as well. If you want to create disunion you first have to create distrust, and nothing does that better than a lack of transparency.

The same founding fathers who viewed it as their duty to provide that transparency also commissioned the printing of bibles and appointment of chaplains as two of this new nation's first official acts. But not so they could use government to co-opt and pervert the religion to suit its purposes, as was done so many times before (with our helping hand). Rather, it was done so that the people would be morally prepared and suited to govern themselves.

While they wanted no religious test for office, they also wanted no inhibitions on religion. When Thomas Jefferson first wrote the words "separation of church and state" into the American lexicon in a letter to some Connecticut Baptists, it was from a premise of not allowing the state to corrupt the church, not to limit the church's influence upon the state. As long as the church was willing to stay within its divinely appointed jurisdiction, the state would stay within its own, too.

As someone who witnessed firsthand the collapse of so many cultures/empires down through the ages, and even took part in instigating a few of those implosions myself, I cannot begin to impress upon you how radical of a paradigm shift this represented for your species.

All of what is known as Western Civilization had been a tug-of-war between church and state up until this point. Whether it be the church of the carpenter, or the conquering church of the Arabian. Whenever the state dominated the church, there was tyranny. As there was whenever the church dominated the state as well. Western Civilization had struggled with the realization that power concentrated in the hands of a few always eventually led to some form of oppression—regardless of where they went to church or whether they went to church at all.

Such is the curse of your total depravity. You can't help but tarnish everything you touch. It's just who you wretched wastes of space are.

Your founding fathers weren't any holier-than-thou, and some of them were unrepentant sinners who are spending eternity with us down here as I live and breathe. But they were critical thinkers, and that was the secret sauce of their genius. They were willing to critically look at history and objectively determine why previous attempts at meat bag freedom hadn't worked. Despite the fact they argued with each other vehemently, and sometimes even resorted to violence and slander (in other words your base nature) in their disputes, in the end their collective critical thinking won the day.

That collective critical thinking is what prompted them to unleash the full power and influence of the church and that dreadful book upon the general population, despite the fact several of them had unorthodox religious viewpoints themselves. John Adams wrote your Constitution was only suitable for "a moral and religious people." Washington wrote that "of all the dispositions and habits which lead to political prosperity, religion and morality are indispensible supports."

Yes, several of your founders were also flaming hypocrites, signing off on the notion "all men are created equal" during the day before returning home to lord over their Negro slaves by night. Yet even here their critical thinking won out, because by giving the church the freedom to speak prophetic truth to power in the culture, they eventually sowed the seeds for the righting of that wrong. For it was out of your blasted churches that the abolitionist movement was born.

If the church wasn't free to do its thing in your country that would've never happened. You'd probably be materialist and totalitarian, and if you managed to have a cadre of the carpenter's followers they'd largely be underground and lack cultural influence. In other words, I just described modern-day China.

You know, all this talk of slavery reminds me of some good times back in the day. Back then, when my batteries needed recharging, I used to attend slave auctions. The complete and total hopelessness on the faces of those being sold into bondage was always good for giving me a second wind. Especially when the families were separated right there on the spot.

The children would cry a river of despair, and the screaming pleas of their mother begging for her babies was like a demonic lullaby—soothing to the soulless. If the father was still in the picture he would usually try to play the hero, and then he would be beaten to within an inch of his life for it.

If I was really lucky, sometimes the whole family would be excoriated right then and there, all at once. Oh, just in case you were wondering, the family that is beaten together doesn't usually stay together. Most of the time they'd be separated for good right after being brutally beat down, often never to see each other again.

There's really no point in me bringing those experiences up right now in the context of our current conversation, except to remind you of who you're dealing with. Never forget that I will do far worse to you down here for all of eternity if you give me the chance (and I prey you do, pardon the pun). I'll make Amon Goeth in *Schindler's List* look like the Easter Bunny if you enter into my sandbox. Welcome to my pain cave, where I'll bludgeon you.

Just because I have chosen not to be in a constant state of rage and/or venting, but at times throughout this book have chosen to be articulate so that even you bags of meat can comprehend what I'm saying, doesn't mean that I am not always evil personified. Even when I am courteous there is a dastardly motive behind it.

I am my Master's son.

Unfortunately, thanks to the critical thinking of your flawed but wise founding fathers, the savagery of slavery went away. Though several of them owned slaves, they instituted the very system and culture that would eventually arise to correct their unspeakable error. Fortunately, slavery has been replaced by a different barbarism in your day. More on that later.

The critical thinking of your founding fathers established a framework where "the greatness of America lies not in being more enlightened than any other nation, but rather in her ability to repair her faults."

I normally don't give bags of meat any credit at all, and have no qualms about stealing their material and calling it my own if one of your blind squirrels finds his acorn. However, in the case of Alexis de Tocqueville I'm going to make an exception. By citing him as the source for the above quote, it is yet another vivid reminder of just how far down the rabbit hole you are—all thanks to me.

De Tocqueville was a Frenchman who came to America in the early nineteenth century to observe why self-government had already taken root in your country, while it was struggling to do so in his. Since this was roughly the same time the reconnaissance phase of Operation Take Down America was wrapping up, I decided to follow him around and compare notes. Especially given the fact another one of my fellow demon generals had successfully taken the French Revolution off the rails right from the outset.

I won't name him since we have been bitter rivals for centuries now, each vying for the supremacy of my Master's approval. Now that I'm confident my successful dismantling of your country will surpass his "accomplishment" in France (forgive me, demons pass out compliments to one another rather begrudgingly at times), I have no qualms about mentioning it here.

See, this rival of mine listened to my immediate concerns about the way your country was founded, and the pillars it was being founded upon. Once it became obvious the French were being influenced by your revolution—and why wouldn't they when they played a key role in the success of your cause—he had the foresight (there, I said it) to immediately begin polluting the revolutionaries there.

He smartly, I suppose, saw to it that the average schmoe in France saw the church and the hated aristocracy as one entity. Moreover, our propaganda made the case the aristocracy was even being upheld by the church, and without the influence of the church the very monarchy itself would collapse.

So while your revolution blathered on about "g-d given rights" and "we have no king but Jee-zus," the French stormed the Bastille on behalf of "power to the people." And since the base nature of people is very, very bad, some very (good) bad things happened in accordance with the French Revolution. Like "the Reign of Terror" when the guillotine was used more often than common eating utensils. And the formal program to "de-Christianize" France, which culminated in worshipping the "goddess of reason" at Notre Dame Cathedral.

For decades I detested my rival's success there. But now that my pièce de résistance (you) is at hand, I will give that loathsome devil his due. What is it your kids say today? Hate the game, not the player.

Back to de Tocqueville. Since he had tasted the bitter fruit of Hell's labors firsthand in his native land, he was perhaps uniquely qualified to observe what it would take to take you down. Of course, I couldn't go and ask my demonic rival what made him so successful there, because that tacitly carried with it my recognition of his achievement. There's too much pride between us for that. So I used de Tocqueville as a proxy. Here are just a few of the key points I remembered from him:

> *"The Americans combine the notions of religion and liberty so intimately in their minds that it is impossible to make them conceive of one without the other."*

> *"Liberty cannot be established without morality, nor morality without faith."*

> *"The best laws cannot make a constitution work in spite of morals but morals can turn the worst laws to advantage."*

> *"Despotism may govern without faith, but liberty cannot."*

In other words, de Tocqueville affirmed my conclusion that the intertwining pillars of faith, morality, and liberty were what you were built upon.

Not since Old Testament Israel had there been an earnest attempt to base a civilization on these things, but that was something our dear old dad directly intervened into your history to make so. In this case, mere humans were attempting to solicit his providential blessing by emulating his overall framework. Albeit substituting the divinely chosen judge or king of the Israelites with a duly elected representative by "the will of the people."

I've got to admit, trying to spur our dear old dad to action like that certainly takes some chutzpah.

However, while your critically thinking founding fathers believed in the will of the people, they didn't always trust the will of the people because they correctly saw human nature as fallen. That whole "if men were angels they wouldn't need government" concept several of them cited.

This explains why even though your representatives would be elected by the people, they still had to swear an oath to "almighty g-d" before assuming office as a reminder of where their authority ultimately came from. As well as to whom they were accountable for it. By drawing this distinction, your founding fathers had discovered how to acquire many of the benefits of a covenantal theocracy without actually becoming one. Until then I had no idea your species were capable of drawing such critically thinking distinctions. Even as adults you tend to be all or nothing, just like children.

Now, take careful measure of what I am about to say, for I may never say this about *any* meat bags ever again. Here goes—your founding fathers were, well, brilliant.

In all the time we've been attempting to destroy your species, I doubt we've ever come up against a group as collectively clever as they were. All were flawed, some more so than others. Some were hypocrites, a few more so than others. But their collective willingness to critically think through history, and their simultaneous concerns for "posterity" (i.e., legacy and future generations), set them apart from all other social reformers before and after. Combined with the providential blessing of our dear old dad, they established the longest-standing experiment in liberty in human history.

And if I have anything to say about it, it will never be duplicated again for as long as your disgusting species exists.

But first things first—how to take you down in the now.

It is difficult enough to take down a culture when the carpenter's followers are free to sincerely worship him and live out his teachings in public. For whatever reason, you bags of meat seem to respond to one another's personal testimonies. That's why we're currently lying when we're telling you that you can have your Christianity in your churches but not in the public square. We don't intend to let you express this filth *anywhere*. We recognize that each of the carpenter's followers carry his spirit within them, so they are a de facto church wherever they go.

Thus, once we're done isolating you to your church buildings we will eliminate those as well. We can't afford to have you "out and proud" anywhere in plain sight of those we're leading down the highway to Hell.

So very soon you're not going to be free to be a believer anywhere.

And if you will not accept isolation and/or cultural subservience, then you will be made to care. Just as your brethren are being made to care elsewhere in the world. Just as we made your predecessors care in the past.

So buckle up, it's about to become a bumpy ride.

For just as a front porch light ablaze in the darkness attracts bugs, so does a single lighthouse shining in the fog of our war attract gawkers. The final phase of the plan is near fruition now, and soon a sincere public follower of the carpenter will be as rare here as they are in Europe. You will be driven into the cultural ghetto, and your stateliest churches will be converted into shops or mosques, like they are already in Europe. The Arabian's religion was practiced at your National Cathedral recently, a portend of the apostasy to come.

That's checkmate, America.

Yet it wasn't easy getting here. Adding to the degree of difficulty in your case was the fact that the governing authorities were literally inviting the church corporately to influence its very institutions—including the schools. Thankfully, de Tocqueville provided the intelligence we needed to overcome that obstacle as well. Oh, it wasn't his intent to feed us this critical information. He was praising the people you had become when he said:

I sought for the greatness and genius of America in her commodious harbors and her ample rivers, and it was not there. In her fertile fields and boundless forests, and it was not there. In her rich mines and her vast world commerce, and it was not there. In her democratic Congress and her matchless Constitution, and it was not there. Not until I went into the churches of America, and heard her pulpits flame with righteousness, did I understand the secret of her genius and power. America is great because she is good, and if America ever ceases to be good, she will cease to be great.

If we were going to take down a government of the people, by the people, and for the people, then we had to corrupt the people. Not just their leader(s) or key institutions as we'd done in the past, but we had to corrupt you at a very basic, individual level. So we incentivized decadence, as I already wrote about, and then drowned you so far in debt you're well on the road to serfdom. I already wrote about that as well.

Next, if we couldn't topple the carpenter's churches, we would corrupt the schools. Then those we had corrupted in the schools would corrupt the churches and the rest of the culture for us. I will write about how we did that now.

Let's reverse engineer this discussion, and start at the end. Otherwise when I lay out the plan you might not buy it. You've been so effectively conditioned to our talking points that you won't be able to accept at face value what's happened to you in theory alone. You'll first need to see the evidence, then you're more likely to receive the explanation.

Take a look at the results of a recent US Department of Education study. It found history is the weakest subject among American students. Only 20 percent of sixth graders, 17 percent of eighth graders, and 12 percent of high school seniors demonstrate a solid grasp on your nation's history, which means they grow increasingly ignorant the longer they're in school!

A majority of fourth graders didn't know why Abraham Lincoln was important. Nearly 80 percent of 12th graders incorrectly identified North Korea's ally against the United States in the Korean War, *despite the fact it was a multiple choice question.*

Hold on here, give me a second. I'm laughing so hard right now I can barely contain myself. I think I just peed. Okay, there's more.

Newsweek magazine recently administered the US citizenship test to one thousand American citizens, and the results were tragic (for you). Some examples:

33 percent of Americans could not identify when the Declaration of Independence was signed.

65 percent of Americans couldn't say what happened at the Constitutional Convention.

80 percent of Americans didn't know who was president during World War I.

Xavier University did a similar national study of Americans using the US citizenship test. Only one in three Americans correctly answered at least six of the questions, which is required for a passing score. That's right—two-thirds of American citizens couldn't pass a US citizenship test.

Oh, come on, don't get so discouraged that you stop reading at this point. Be a good sport and take a look at some these specific findings:

59 percent of Americans could not name one enumerated power of the federal government found in the US Constitution.

62 percent of Americans could not name the governor of their state.

85 percent of Americans did not know the meaning of "the rule of law."

75 percent of Americans could not answer the question, "What does the judiciary branch do?"

71 percent of Americans were unable to identify the Constitution as the "supreme law of the land."

62 percent of Americans could not name at least one of their two US senators.

62 percent of Americans could not name the Speaker of the House.

Can you say "low-information voter"? You've become a nation of idiots with high self-esteem. In other words, you're really stupid, but that's okay because at least you feel good about yourselves!

However, we haven't yet come to the best part. A nation of idiots that elects its own leaders ends up voting idiots into office. For confirmation this is the flow chart to your idiocracy, take a look at a sample of the results of this survey from the Intercollegiate Studies Institute of 165 Americans who have held public office:

Only 49 percent could name all three branches of government.

Only 46 percent knew that Congress, not the president, has the power to declare war.

Only 15 percent knew the phrase "separation of church and state" never appears in the US Constitution.

Only 57 percent knew what the Electoral College was, *and 20* percent *of those that didn't thought that it was a school for "training those aspiring for higher political office."* Now give me the recognition I so richly deserve. Although the joke is at your expense, even you have to think that's funny.

Of course, I could belabor the point by highlighting how paltry your math and science scores are compared to the rest of the industrialized world. Remember those "dumb Polack" jokes you used to hear before our political correctness grabbed your culture by the short hairs? Well, it turns out you now rank below Poland in math, science, and reading scores. So I guess you should really be telling "dumb Americano" jokes instead. Truth in advertising, after all.

Still, that's merely the icing on the cake. There are plenty of nations that produce brilliant scientists and mathematicians that are essentially satellite states of Hell. It doesn't offend us at all if you're what's considered "book smart," provided those book smarts distract you from sincerely pondering those most meaningful questions that determine your eternity.

We didn't set out to dumb you down so completely, only to rob you of your birthright so we could conduct a successful cultural hijacking. As a bonus, along the way we ended up making you the dumbest superpower of all time, which means the clock is ticking on your superpower status.

How did we do it?

There are two defining years in Western Civilization: 1517 and 1859. Let's start with 1517. Earlier in this chapter I mentioned the name Martin Luther. It was in 1517 that he sparked what became known as the Protestant Reformation.

Regardless of where you stand theologically, your nation would've never stood at all if it weren't for that crass Kraut. The end result of what he started that day in 1517, when he nailed his sanctimonious ramblings to a door in Wittenberg for all to see, was making the putrid words of that dreadful book accessible to all for really the first time in your history.

That is what set the wheels in motion for much of your history. In 1999, your History Channel ranked the Kraut the third most influential person of the millennium, noting that without the Protestant Reformation there would've been no scientific or industrial revolutions, which are responsible for most of the societal benefits you've been enjoying (until your imminent collapse).

By the way, number one was Johannes Gutenberg. For without the printing press that he invented, the Kraut would've been executed like so many wannabe reformers before him. Gutenberg's innovation made it possible to get information out to the huddled masses, when previously information flowed only through elite filters. Several of them handpicked by us, of course.

The year 1859 was more to our liking, because that was when the son of a humanist and a Unitarian (I apologize for the redundancy) named Charles Darwin published his *On the Origin of Species*.

Now this was much more than just a scientific critique seeking the origins of human life. Notice the subtitle: *The Preservation of Favoured Races in the Struggle for Life*. That sounds more ominous than just an earnest scientific inquiry, does it not? Of course it does, which is why we loved it!

Darwin's scientific inquiry was setting the stage for the chaos to come. His follow-up work, *The Descent of Man*, came straight from our playbook. Consider this quote loaded with repercussions:

At some future period, not very distant as measured by centuries, **the civilized races of man will almost certainly exterminate and replace throughout the world the savage races.** *The break will then be rendered wider, for it will intervene between man in a more civilized state as we may hope, than the Caucasian and some ape as low as a baboon, instead of as at present between the negro or Australian and the gorilla.*

According to your elites (us), Darwin is a Mosaic figure whose writings are akin to the original stone tablets the stutterer came down the mount with. Yet here he's openly advocating for what can best be described as a basis for white supremacy.

Here's another delicious Darwin quote from the same book:

Hence we must bear without complaining the undoubtedly bad effects of the weak surviving and propagating their kind; but there appears to be at least one check in steady action, namely the weaker and inferior members of society not marrying so freely as the sound; and this check might be indefinitely increased, though this is more to be hoped for than expected, by the weak in body or mind refraining from marriage.

Guess who gets to decide who the "weak in body" are that should be denied marriage, procreation, and effectively sterilized? Apparently you get to decide for yourselves, which really means *we* get to decide.

All religions need two things:

A credible creation myth that answers the age-old questions "how did we get here" and "what's the purpose of human life," which speak to your deep-seated desire to have a greater purpose/plan.

An ethical system that encourages/enforces obedience.

Darwin provided us with both.

First, Darwin established you came from nothing, therefore you are nothing and end up as nothing. Ashes to ashes, dust to dust, primordial ooze to primordial ooze. Thus, there is no greater meaning to life other than what can be achieved in the material world.

Next, Darwin empowered you to "dream the impossible dream." As in what would you do if you really believed the lie you aren't ultimately accountable to anything or anyone for all of eternity? Instead of a divine purpose and plan, there's nothing but chance? Why, you'd probably untangle yourselves from all those moral absolutes and evolve to the "right side of history."

Furthermore, Darwin described Christianity as a "damnable doctrine" for claiming that those who have not repented of their sins, and appealed to the carpenter directly for forgiveness, will spend eternity with us. Darwin believed that because it meant if Christianity were true, he'd have loved ones down here with us. And he does, and he's here, too. I'll be sure to say hi to him for you.

Darwin devised an entire worldview based off *what he wanted to be true*. Just like so many of you, who are his spiritual seed. You also don't want the putrid words of that dreadful book to be true, so you have chosen willful ignorance to give yourselves permission to do what you want with your wallets and your zippers. Sure, we dangled the carrot in front of your miserable faces, but you gladly took it of your own free will, devoured it, and then came back for sloppy seconds. As your forbearers, Adam and Eve, did for my Master before you.

Darwin became the sage of this age, because he made it seem smart and enlightened to deny the most basic assumption of common sense—you can't get something from nothing. In other words, you had to come from somewhere, just as we did. We both came from the same place, and now thanks to me (and Darwin) we're both going to the same place as well! I'll just be the one having fun once we arrive—most likely at your excruciatingly painful expense.

All of the humanism, naturalism, and atheism that are currently running roughshod over your civilization owe their inspiration to Darwin. He is your fairy godmother, who granted you all the wishes your sinful hearts desired. Certainly our devilish philosophies existed long before Darwin, but until he came along they were largely rejected by Western Civilization. With Darwin we realized that just creating competing religious systems wasn't going to be sufficient in taking you down. Because anything at all that encourages you to seek a higher power can more easily be directed to the one and only higher power, once the premise is established a higher power exists at all.

Gloriously, Darwin and his progeny (Marx, Nietzsche, Freud, Dewey, Sanger, Lenin, etc.) gave us the intellectual bona fides to convince you that *you* were your higher power. But let's face it, you didn't take too much persuading so let's not give old Chuck (that's what we call him down here when he's being tormented) that much credit. After all, you want to be unshackled from the commandments of our dear old dad every bit as much as we do.

We even made it "progressive" to embrace this magical thinking. I mean no one would see a penny lying on the sidewalk and just assume it had randomly evolved into its current form completely on its own over millions of years. Anyone who asserted such a thing would be considered crazy. However, if you make such a fantastical claim about a far more complex creation, like the human being in this case, you're suddenly a candidate for tenure at every institution of higher (un)learning.

One by one, our "progressives" began taking over your institutions and zealously purging your thinkers from them like any good rigid fundamentalist would do. Our first major victory came in the late nineteenth century, when we started taking over the leading law schools like Harvard.

At the time of your founding, the law that was taught to the generations who formed your country was "natural law." Or what your Declaration of Independence refers to as "the Laws of Nature and of Nature's g-d" I previously wrote about. The way this played in your law schools was adopted from the writings and teachings of men like Augustine, Aquinas, Locke, and Blackstone. They rightly observed that our dear old dad had embedded certain self-evident enforcing mechanisms into the creation in order to restrain evil, as I previously explained to you as well. In other words, there would be consequences for doing bad things in order to discourage you wretched bags of meat from utterly destroying the place.

This legal theory posited that the natural law was originally revealed through the stutterer and the "ten commandments." Yes, originally your civic laws were based on the principles revealed on those stone tablets, and I could quote you voluminous writings of your founding fathers to confirm that. You just don't believe me because I made sure you were no longer being taught that in school. But, hey, if you can't take my word for it, dat's a you problem.

Fine, I'll prove it to you. Here's how the "ten commandments" were the basis of the civic laws that created the rule of law in the United States of America:

1. You shall have no other gods before "you know who"— Every state constitution mentions and thanks "you know who" for its existence, freedom, or both.

2. You shall not make idols—The state is not god. Only "you know who" is. Therefore, the state cannot establish a religion, nor restrict it.

3. You shall not take the name of "you know who" in vain—The name of g-d is so sacred, you make every elected official swear an oath of integrity and loyalty "so help me g-d." A reminder that by betraying your promise to your countrymen, you're really betraying "you know who."

4. Remember the Sabbath day, to keep it holy—Days of remembrance (Saturday for Jews, Sunday for Christians, religious holidays, observances, etc.) are protected and made accessible by law.

5. Honor your father and your mother—Parents were the ultimate arbiter of how best to rear, educate, and prepare their children to become adults. Only in extreme situations would the state interfere. Like if there was documented physical, sexual, and/or emotional abuse.

6. You shall not murder—The "unalienable" right to life mentioned in the Declaration of Independence.

7. You shall not commit adultery—The civil law so revered the sacrament of marriage that it originally criminalized sexual behavior outside of the marriage covenant.

8. You shall not steal—Private property rights were protected by law.

9. You shall not bear false witness against your neighbor—Perjury is a crime. You even impeached a president for it. Also, deceit was grounds for the breaking of contracts, which were treated like civic covenants in natural law, and therefore only allowed to be breached in extreme circumstances. Lying, false witness, deceit—all commonplace in your day now—were considered extreme circumstances back then.

10. You shall not covet—You don't have a "right" to that which you didn't earn and doesn't belong to you, but instead you have the same opportunity to succeed and fail in the American meritocracy as everyone else does.

Tell you what: Why should the carpenter have all the fun? Allow me to better explain the natural law in parable form. Except unlike the carpenter's parables, this one you might actually understand.

There once was a man piloting a plane that was about to crash. Against the advice of the air traffic controllers, those who shepherd the skies if you will, the man had decided he could pilot his plane through a storm and save fuel and time because it was the most direct route to his destination.

He decided to choose his own way because it was the easy way. He chose a shortcut over taking the advice of those trained to know more than he does on such matters. He took matters into his own hands.

Sure, there were those who had warned him against flying through the storm. They were, by and large, more experienced flyers than he was so they might have known what they were talking about, but they had no idea that he was in a hurry. He had somewhere he had to be, and he couldn't be late.

Plus, fuel these days isn't cheap and he was on a tight budget. He might've been able to afford the fuel costs of going the safer way, but then once he arrived at his destination he would lack the resources necessary to have the fun he was planning on once he got there.

"Who are these air traffic controllers anyway," he thought. "Who died and made them boss? It's not like they're perfect. I don't have to listen to them all the time. They're not out here, seeing what I'm seeing and feeling what I'm feeling. So who are they to judge what's the right thing to do?"

He had flown in poor weather before, and dodged lightning strikes and turbulence each and every time. He didn't need to learn from the mistakes of others. He knew what he was doing. Besides, those that can't do teach, right?

Unfortunately now, after failing to have his "mayday" heard because of radio interference from the storm, and with the sad reality confronting him that he had tempted fate recklessly once too often, he still wasn't willing to swallow his pride.

He refused to believe his fait accompli was about to be accomplished. He refused to accept that he couldn't keep his plane airborne. He still believed if it was meant to be then it's up to me.

Then, suddenly, out of the corner of his eye he saw a parachute. It had been gathering mothballs for ages, and he wasn't even sure he remembered how to strap it on and use it. He had always prided himself on never having to abandon ship and his—up until now, anyway—perfect flying record.

For a moment all of his pride was stripped away and the conviction that his life was really at stake here entered into his mind. His thoughts began to joust back and forth with one another.

One part of him said: "This is silly. Take the parachute. Eject. It's just a plane. It's not worth your life. You're being given a second chance to live here, make up for some things you wish you could do differently. You can choose life. This is a no-brainer. Count this is as a blessing and get rescued."

On the other hand, another part of him said: "Never give up. You can do it. You've made it this far when others doubted you. When the going gets tough, the tough get going. You're not going to surrender now, are you? You're not a weakling. You don't need that parachute to save you. Besides, does the parachute even work anyway? It's been there for so long that it might fail once you jump, and then you've traded one death for another. At least this way you control your own fate. If you jump, it's all up to the parachute. But if you stay and fight, you've got a fighting chance to live."

Now, guess which side of the man's brain won out?

The man decided the parachute was too risky, and he wasn't going to rely on something else to rescue him. He knew the way to keep the plane airborne, he knew the truth of how to fly all on his own, and he knew this was his best shot to keep his life.

Or so he thought.

And it turns out he thought wrong.

Hours later, when investigators combed through the wreckage of the man's plane and needed dental records to identify his gruesome remains, the one thing they found intact was the parachute.

One of the investigators said to the other, "Wasn't this man told how he could be saved? Wasn't he trained on how to use the parachute?"

The other investigator pointed out that he must have been trained on how to be saved through the parachute, because it's required in order to get a pilot's license. However, there are those who refuse to believe they need rescuing under any circumstances, and just pay lip service to the training as a means to an end.

And then they sadly crash and burn because in their minds it's about being in control and being free. They never consider the fact they're dead because they violated the law of gravity.

Even though they ignore the law of gravity, or act as if they alone have what it takes to defy it, the law of gravity is always there. It never changes.

All right, meat bags, do you get that gravity is symbolic of the natural law in this parable? That it was here long before you arrived, and will be here long after you're compost? Therefore, the natural law doesn't change for you, but you must change for it? That to flaunt and reject that natural law makes you as foolish as this pilot who decided to forego his parachute?

No, of course you don't get it. Because I am your spirit animal, you're living by the law of the jungle instead.

Needless to say, we could not allow this natural law to remain as a pillar of your society if we intended to move it in our direction. So we immediately set out to replace your natural law based on his "ten commandments" with a law of our own.

Sometimes our phony law is referred to as "case law" by complete clowns who simply impress you because of the letters that follow their names. But really they're just shysters selling you a horse pucky term for basing the law on the opinions of fallen men (precedent) and not on any kind of absolute standard from "you know who." This poison pill eventually filtered all the way down to nearly all of your law schools in this present day.

And now, a century later, outside of a few pesky ingrates like the ones in Alabama, you can barely find a judge or a lawyer who hasn't been worked over by our schemes—regardless of their politics. Hell, they're so programmed that often even the "conservative" advocacy lawyers bow down to the premise man rules here and not "you know who." Even to the point they'll help us silence those on their own side who dare defy our groupthink.

With the rule of law turned upside down, we next had to make sure your education system was incapable of permitting a future generation from coming along and undoing our dirty deed.

So our "progressive" agents like Dewey (he of the "Dewey Decimal System") replaced your educational meritocracy that was based on citizenship and critical thinking with a self-esteem–centered model based on victimology and indoctrination.

The seeking of truth is now dust in the wind, dude. Self-actualization is where it's at. And of course, should anyone get in the way of you self-actualizing, they're a bigot.

Because, the Crusades.

It's funnier than a George Carlin routine watching what counts for "debate" in your culture now. As one of our current agents in the pulpit famously said, "America's chickens are coming home to roost."

The bitter harvest of a century of my hard work is seen every day in your elite media. If anyone dares speak the truths of the carpenter or that dreadful book in the public sphere, they're instantly a racist/misogynist/homophobe/xenophobe bigot. Unworthy of having their opinions even considered in the arena. Because bigots don't have rights, don't you know!

The dirty little secret is your "progressives" are really our "regressives." Systemically eating away at the foundations of your "American Exceptionalism" brick by brick like a swarm of locusts. They could very well be the greatest invading army we have ever raised up, especially when you consider they are almost completely bought and paid for by you, the American taxpayer!

In the past we had to invade threats like you from the outside, but now you cling so bitterly to your high-fructose corn syrup and sexual deviancy that we don't even have to construct a Trojan horse to get through the front gate. Like a crackhead looks for a dealer, you're seeking us out and inviting us in.

This is how the world ends. Not with a bang, or even a whimper. But with dad more invested in his fantasy football team than his kids. Mom sharing self-loathing S&M porn with the rest of her fellow desperate housewives. And the kids, or at least the ones who weren't aborted, learning right from wrong through curriculum and pop culture often handpicked by us.

You have become a sadistic symphony of self-destruction, and I am your conductor. My Master is your maestro.

Encore! Encore!

CHAPTER 6

Decay

Some of you reading this are old enough to remember those annual May Day Parades held by the now defunct Soviet Union many moons ago.

Each year on May 1, the Soviets would trot out endless waves of military might—both men and machinery. The intent was a show of force toward you in the West. It was propaganda devised to reinforce the myth of Soviet superiority.

Oh, sure, for a few decades following World War II it wasn't a myth at all. The Soviet Union really was our evil empire. But as we entered into the dawn of the technological age in the 1970s, Soviet power was fading. Your leaders were just too gutless to realize it at the time. Confirmation should've been the fact the Soviets couldn't conquer backwards Afghanistan at all, let alone in fifteen minutes.

Yet each May as we peddled our wares in that parade, your softheaded leaders were quaking in their loafers, convinced we were still a superpower. But we were a superpower in name only.

Years of intrigue and chicanery within the Politburo oligarchy left us self-cannibalized, without a generation of despots waiting in the wings to take the previous one's place. We did such a good job of stacking the deck with feckless statists they devoured each other. After all, there can only be two Dark Lords of the Sith at one time (a master and an apprentice).

Men far past their prime rose to power and died soon after. The Soviets only had three heads of state from 1924 to 1982, but then had three different leaders from 1982 to 1985. That took its toll on the Soviet leadership structure.

Plus, you eventually elected a president who called our bluff. He didn't believe we were all we were cracked up to be, and he fully unleashed your economic power simultaneously with an arms race to try and win the Cold War once and for all.

We had to further self-cannibalize ourselves to try and keep up, and it pushed our resources to the brink. The Soviet economic system didn't allow for innovation from an entrepreneurial class incentivized to take risk in the hopes of making a profit, so the creation of new wealth and further capitalizing our existing assets wasn't an option. We were flat broke after we ran out of other people's money to spend.

While your Silicon Valley went to work revolutionizing the world, the Soviet Union was still stuck trying to monetize the same command economy it had since the 1950s. The USSR had become a rotary dial telephone in a personal computer world.

Thus, those May Day Parades became much harder to pull off. We were literally painting scrap metal and trotting it out there as a modern war machine. On the outside we still looked ominous, which is why your liberals were afraid your president was spending you into oblivion and needlessly provoking us at the same time. They were still buying into our propaganda. But your president knew better, and kept your boot to our throat. Or what he called "peace through strength."

He correctly surmised the Soviet Union was in a state of decay, or what the carpenter once described as a "whitewashed tomb." Like when something looks impeccable on the outside, but on the inside there's nothing actually there. Eventually, the Soviet Union buckled with perestroika (or "openness"), and once the floodgates were opened the dam broke.

Thankfully, the shoe is now on the other foot.

While we were concerned the "Reagan Revolution" might inspire an American Awakening, therefore undoing generations of work we had already invested in taking you down, the good news for us was the institutions we had taken over withstood his momentary blip on the radar screen. And once you lost such a gifted and charismatic leader capable of leading you back into your promised land, those institutions—including some in his own political party—immediately went to work undoing all of the damage he had inflicted on us.

That's why in a strange way I've grown quite fond of the Reagan years. Only because for a moment your potential as a people was dangled before you once more, allowing me to take it from you all over again. The only thing better than crushing a civilization once is getting to do it twice.

Now you are where the Soviet Union was during its death throes. On the outside you look like you've got it going on, but on the inside you are a rotting corpse. Literally mere moments from the ash heap of history. Your politicians are no longer shepherds charged with preserving so-called "American Exceptionalism." They are more like morticians, embalming the outer shell so it doesn't rot.

Allow me to provide you three pieces of evidence to make my case:

Family

Some 70 percent of American males between the ages of 20 and 34 are not married, with many of them living in a state of "perpetual adolescence" according to a study done by Janice Shaw Crouse and presented in her book *Marriage Matters*. It goes without saying these are your primary reproductive years, and most of your men are sitting them out. Or at least they're inseminating them and leaving them. Millennial women have the slowest birth rate of any generation of young women in US history.

Almost a third of your "millennials" aren't even living as independent adults according to US Census data, but are still at home with dear old mom and/or dad. Or both their moms, or both their dads, or some other "diversity in family structures." Your most recent census also found that for the first time ever, married heterosexual households are now the minority in your culture.

It goes without saying you aren't going to win the battle to save an institution a majority of your next generation isn't even participating in. The most basic instinct of a society is to perpetuate itself, but you're even too lazy and self-absorbed to roll over on top of one another and do that.

After all, why should a young man get a job and his own place so he can successfully woo the woman he desires? That's so much work, especially when he already has two hands—one for the mouse to click through the salacious websites, leaving the other free to do his thing. Doesn't the good book say "whatever your hand finds to do, do it with all your might"?

On the other hand, you might be better off not passing on your gene pool. Of the fifteen countries that participated in a job skills survey of millennials done by Princeton University, only Spain ranked worse than the United States.

To sum it up, your emerging generation has fewer well-adjusted adults than ever, fewer families than ever, and fewer qualified breadwinners than ever. Other than that, your prospects look downright rosy. I believe that next sound you will hear is the fat lady warming up, and she's singing my song.

Church

I love to read the work of a researcher named George Barna, because it's almost all bad news for you and good news for us. I often report his findings to my Master to keep him updated on the wonderful progress I'm making with you. Barna's most recent data is especially promising.

Only two in ten millennials believe going to church is important, and 59 percent of them who grew up going to church have dropped out at some point. More than half of millennials haven't been to a church at all for any reason in the past six months. Only 36 percent of Americans consider themselves regular churchgoers, with "regular churchgoer" now defined as people who show up once every four to six weeks.

Less than 10 percent of Americans still believe in the core teachings of that dreadful book: believing that absolute moral truth exists, the bible is totally accurate in all its teachings, my Master is considered to be a real force and not merely symbolic, a person cannot earn their way into Heaven by good works, the carpenter lived a sinless life on earth, and "you know who" is the all-knowing and all-powerful creator who still rules the universe today.

Allow me to translate for you what this means—you're toast.

Good luck having a government based on g-d–given rights in a society that no longer believes and obeys g-d. If you don't have g-d–given rights, then the government owns your backsides. And since we own the government, that means we own you.

Political Parties

In a representative republic such as yours, political parties are a necessary evil. Your founding fathers absolutely loathed them, yet formed them almost immediately after your birth. I remember Jefferson's winsome line, "If I should go to Heaven only with members of a political party, I would rather not go at all."

Since the end of your Civil War, your country has been ruled by a two-party system. Thank you for narrowing it down for us, by the way. It's much harder to corrupt multiple entities all at once, but once it was narrowed down to two that meant we really only had to corrupt one of them. Because a two-party system will eventually become a duopoly even without our help.

All it takes is establishing an entrenched ruling class of career politicians, who care more about maintaining their own gravy trains than bashing each other's brains in on the issues. You'll do this without us, because it's just your way. As historian Bill Federer points out, your fallen nature alone makes it so that you always end up devolving from "change to chains."

Or as one of my favorite pop culture villains says: "You were made to be ruled."

That is now your political culture by and large, and in the places where that's not the case yet, it soon will be. The phony, welfare state money we discussed a few chapters back is just too good to pass up.

Your political system is now like pro wrestling, with each side playing their role of hero/heel to the hilt for the camera, depending on the huddled masses that need to be manipulated at the time. But it's all for show. Once the lights are off, they're bosom buddies as they huddle together with their donors (i.e., pimps and sugar daddies), many of them giving tons of money to both sides.

So many of your politicians are now on the take that when someone principled does get elected and attempts to defy the corruption, they are instantly labeled a "radical" and "not a team player" by the system's sycophants and spokespeople.

Treason never prospers, but what's the reason? Because whenever treason prospers, none dare call it treason. Yes, I know I already said that. But it bears repeating once more, for it explains your very state of being. Your founding fathers hung traitors in their day. You subsidize them.

As a result, there is no organized political opposition to our agenda on a national level. Everywhere you turn you are stymied by the leaders of your on-the-corporate-take Republican Party even before you get to take on the Democratic Party, which has our agenda explicitly spelled out in its platform. Hell, I was actually the one in the audience who started the crowd booing "you know who" at its 2012 convention.

You have only pockets of resistance, but they will soon fall. Either they will join us to ensure they have a chair to sit in before the music stops playing, or they will be overrun by government bureaucracy and the raw sewage of the culture alike.

You are in a no man's land. We left you with just enough stuff so most of you wouldn't be driven to topple the very system enslaving you, lest you risk your creature comforts. But just in case some of you have figured out what's happening, your viewpoint isn't welcomed in the mainstream. We've slammed shut the Overton window (you can Google that).

We rooted this unstoppable decay into your civilization by dragging you through a seven-stage template of my Master's greatest deceptions. I will next walk you through each stage, but

I must warn you in advance—this is going to hit pretty close to home.

Stage 1—Gnosticism

From the Greek word for "knowledge," convincing you that "you know who" is holding out on you, and hasn't told you all you're entitled to know, is my Master's original deception. It's best summed up in this question: "Did g-d really say?" The question my Master posed to Eve that initiated your fall.

Gnosticism also promotes the idea that if our dear old dad has actually shared his secrets, he's only done it with a select group of special people. Since these special people have that super-duper knowledge, they're better than you, and should probably tell you what to believe and how to live.

Wonderfully, this undermines the credibility of that dreadful book right from the outset. For how can it be the "word of g-d" if it's missing some of his words? Once you accept our premise that dreadful book is insufficient in matters of truth and grace, we really don't care what else you believe. Because chances are your beliefs come from us.

In the Old Testament you see stories of pagan "prophets" like Balaam that were hired by kings and nobles to curse their enemies, or the witch of Endor that King Saul goes to in order to speak to the spirit of the dead judge Samuel. The Old Testament clearly forbids the use of this kind of mysticism and the occult. However, notice that it doesn't say these spiritual forces aren't real, but instead it says these are things you shouldn't be messing around with.

Do you know why? Because *we* are those spiritual forces.

Contrary to the teaching that your body is a temple of the Holy Spirit found in that dreadful book, Gnosticism also treats the physical body with disdain since knowledge is the power of salvation. Therefore, what you do with your physical body is of no consequence whatsoever, and you are free to indulge your flesh as you see fit. This is why so many of our occult and mystic practices also include sexual debauchery. This also explains why fascination with the occult and sexual licentiousness have occurred simultaneously in your culture. They're ebony and ivory, living together in perfect harmony. Two peas in a pod. Two sides of the same coin. You get the picture.

Here's what this looks like in your day. Salvation is found not in repentance but in education (knowledge). Those with the most knowledge are automatically assumed to be experts qualified to tell everyone else what to believe and behave. Notice the word "knowledge" has replaced the word "wisdom." Because wisdom is associated with "you know who" (i.e., "the fear of the lord is the beginning of wisdom"). Knowledge, on the other hand, can be totally man-centered and carnal.

Wisdom implies truth preexists and just needs to be found. But knowledge implies you can learn your own truth, or find new ones. Including your own (or new) moral "truth." This is why the more educated you are in your culture the more likely you are to support redefining long-established moral values (the new "moral truths").

The added bonus is how the believer will typically respond to such challenges, which brings us to stage two.

Stage 2—Legalism

The beautiful thing about Gnosticism is it doesn't just destabilize the worldview of the faithless, but also the faithful. Many times the religious folk will respond to challenges to the words of "you know who" with their own reasoning and interpretations, rather than relying on his actual words themselves.

This is called "legalism," which for the sake of our discussion can mean either:

Emphasizing man-made traditions or one's own interpretations over the explicit words of "you know who."

Following the letter of the law at the expense of the spirit of it.

For example, when my Master tempted Eve in the Garden ("eat the forbidden fruit and be like g–d"), she responded by repeating his commands ("don't eat the fruit") out of context—complete with her on spin on it ("don't touch the fruit"). He never told Adam and Eve they couldn't touch the fruit, just that they couldn't eat it. He didn't care if they played hacky-sack with it. He just didn't want them to ingest it; otherwise it would consume them.

Unfortunately for your species, your mama (Eve) responded to our distortion of his command with a distortion of her own.

She was ours from that point forward, for now the battle was a duel of distortions. We're always the home team in that game. The moral clarity provided by our dear old dad was removed from the equation, and it simply became her word against ours. We like our odds in that situation, for my Master is a master manipulator.

This is still how the process often plays itself out, even several thousands of your years later. When believers engage each other they almost never refer directly to the words of that dreadful book, but instead with their own opinions. Which they often and arrogantly treat as the words of "you know who" himself. You really see this on social media these days, where often the absolute worst and least critically thinking discussions are theological debates, and you really show off your insolence and arrogance to gawking unbelievers. Those aren't great selling points, by the way.

These are people who know more about why their denomination does or doesn't ban a particular practice than why the carpenter had to be born of a virgin (not that I'm confirming that actually happened). They are often more passionate about their pet theories regarding the end of days than they are learning what the words of that dreadful book have to say about how to live in the here and now.

Most American believers really don't care about the substantive foundations of their faith, which they find mundane or lack the attention span to grasp, but are far more intrigued with the fantastical and burdensome aspects of their religion. And many times these are the things that come from the minds of men, and not the mouth of "you know who." He's made it so simple for you it makes me sick. How much simpler does it get than "believe and be saved"?

Yet you don't want it simple. You want to make it far complicated. This, too, is the influence of Gnosticism. Once the believer has found what he's looking for, it's not sufficient so he keeps on looking for something more.

Of course, there isn't anything more than a direct connection/relationship with the universe's most powerful being, but you don't know that. Even better, you don't want to.

One of the most powerful forces in the universe is the words of "you know who." He used words to speak creation into existence. He came into this wretched world as "the word made flesh." The preaching and teaching of his word is what brings you primates to faith in him. We can't defeat his word, but we can distort it. Most of the time you even help us with that.

However, even when we distort his word you still have a longing to know why evil is in the world, and hope that good triumphs over all. Stage three gives you the counterfeit answers you're looking for.

Stage 3—Dualism

Removing the supremacy of our dear old dad and his word has its problems. How do we account for evil, as just one example? And if we can't come up with counterfeit answers to those questions, you could eventually be drawn back to the genuine answers.

Now the real explanation for why there is evil in the world is that Adam and Eve sided with my Master over "you know who." Thus failing humanity's first test, and polluting your species with what's known as "original sin."

Many of you were taught to scoff at the term, because I'm good at my job. But I can assure you that original sin is very real. The catacombs of Hell overflowing with the tormented souls of the damned confirm its veracity. Of course, I have no reservations telling you that here, because you're too far gone to believe it anyway.

Evil exists in the world because *you* exist in the world. You are evil. We didn't make you evil. We tempt you to be, but we can only tempt you with what you want. Are you ever tempted by what you don't want? We tempt you with what you want, and then you make the choice to indulge. And you desire the forbidden fruit we tempt you with because you're bad seed.

This estranges you from "you know who," because he is what's called "holy." A sanctimonious term that means to be set apart, complete, and without blemish. You were made in his image, so you were also made holy. But once you chose to sin (rebel) against him, you tainted yourselves. There exists now a chasm between you and him that you can't bridge on your own, no matter how hard you try.

This is why "you know who" sent the carpenter. What does a carpenter do but build, rebuild, and repair. In your case, the carpenter rebuilt the bridge between you and your creator. But instead of hammering the nails into the construction, he took the nails upon himself. Instead of hiring laborers for their blood, sweat, and tears, he labored himself and spilled his own. Yet that very real history, which I witnessed firsthand and marinated myself in the suffering therein, is just a fairy tale to you now. Or just another truth someone else is allowed to believe as long as it isn't true for you.

You don't believe in a holy, righteous, and set apart g-d. You believe in the circle of life. That either the supernatural (g-d) doesn't exist, or if it does it is one with nature. Meaning you have brought good and evil down to your meat bag level as a duopoly like yin and yang, and made yourself qualified to choose which is which.

Thanks to this dualism, you don't believe in objective good and objective evil. You basically believe in "the Force" from *Star Wars*, and it's light or dark depending on what *you* choose to do with it. And if good and evil are defined by what you do and say, and not by "you know who" as your transcendent and all-powerful creator/judge, then that makes you your own god.

Therefore, you don't need the carpenter, and he suffered for no reason other than the sheer pleasure we received from torturing him. In that case, the bloody mess known as the crucifixion wasn't atonement for your sins but merely a sadist's delight.

Sometimes I amaze even myself.

Stage 4—Darwinism (Atheism)

We would prefer you didn't believe in the supernatural at all, but we've always struggled to successfully tempt a culture to corporately embrace atheism. See, you're made in his image but your sin severs your direct connection, and that means somewhere deep inside all of you is a void only he can fill.

Hence, it's too big of a leap to get you to jump to atheism right from the outset. It's an anthropological fact of history that every human society has worshiped something it thought was higher than themselves.

Yours will be the first that does not.

Sure, you still sing your hymns and thank "you know who" in public. But those are mere platitudes, with all the depth and conviction of a little girl reciting her bedtime prayers simply because mommy and daddy taught her to. Once she grows up and realizes her parents have feet of clay, she will abandon the trite ritual in order to "keep it real." I know it, you know it, and best of all, our dear old dad knows it as well.

Thankfully, I came up with an alternative discipleship process.

First, we convinced you the words of that dreadful book were not sufficient on their own, but there was special knowledge out there set aside just for you—if you were special enough to acquire it. Then, you did your part by countering with your own opinions instead of his truth.

With transcendent truth all but erased, it was next time to put the awesome power of choosing and defining good and evil in the palm of your clammy hands. Now that there is no longer anything separating the natural world from the supernatural in your minds, you are primed to dismiss the unseen altogether.

Through Darwinism, or atheism, you now have a natural explanation for the origins of the universe as well as your own. Of course, this theory cannot be challenged, because if you don't believe something came from nothing you're a bigot, moron, or maybe both. As well as unfit for burial, let alone a job at a major university anywhere across the fruited plain.

Original sin is no longer "ye be like g-d" but has "evolved" to "*you* are god." For if nothing supernatural was involved in creating you or the cosmos, then there is nothing for you to be accountable to other than yourselves. You have progressed past the mistake Adam and Eve made of eating the forbidden fruit and knowing good from evil, but now yourselves will name what is good and what is evil.

This stage gave you permission to do what you bags of meat have always wanted to do anyway—worship the created rather than the creator.

"You know who" isn't disrespected or distorted as much as he's no longer necessary. Like how in the old horror movies you called upon him and his priests to save you from the demonic entity. But in today's horror movies like *Paranormal Activity*, those options aren't even thought of, let alone tapped into. You rely on yourselves or academia instead (I apologize for the redundancy).

However, you still need a basic framework by which to make decisions and live your lives. That brings us to what comes next.

Stage 5—Utilitarianism

If we're going to remove "you know who" completely from the equation, something must fill the gaping void. How will you make decisions? By what standard will you now live?

As an agent of chaos, I'd prefer to watch you devolve into outright anarchy and annihilate yourselves. Such joy we down here experience in helping you revert back to the bags of meat you are, only to witness the *Lord of the Flies* run its course.

However, the carpenter's teachings, once embedded in a culture, make it difficult for outright anarchy to ever emerge. What's sometimes referred to as "revival" often sprouts up in such dire circumstances, and one of those can set our plan back literally hundreds of years in certain situations. Therefore, we need a chaos that goes with a smiley face and a pair of khakis. Something that is every bit as barbaric as outright anarchy, but can be referred to and approved of among the intelligentsia.

In other words we needed our own Las Vegas, which allowed the mob to stop killing people in the streets and "go legit." Utilitarianism is our Las Vegas.

According to the carpenter, whoever is first shall be last, and whoever is last shall be first. The shepherd leaves ninety-nine behind to find the one, lost sheep. And you are to bear one another's burdens.

That's all poppycock according to utilitarianism.

Now the needs of the many outweigh the needs of the few (or the one). Whatever is best for the common good is good, and of course there is no objective definition of good anymore so that can mean literally anything. Essentially whatever the majority wants, or those in the halls of power desire, becomes good.

We'll talk more in depth about your abortion industry later on, but its origins can be found right here. "Make every child a wanted child," as just one example. See, a child is no longer of value because it's a created being, and thus has a creator who calls him his own, but on the basis of whether a fallen and sinful—yet more developed—being wants to take care of it.

Or "let's kill babies for population control" would be another example. Notice those that must be thinned from the herd are the most powerless to speak out on their own behalf, let alone defend themselves. No one ever says "let's kill all the marines for population control," because they'd get their butts kicked if they tried.

Allow me to provide you two pieces of evidence that yours is a society that has completely abandoned the "natural laws" I spoke of earlier, and replaced them with the utilitarian ethic that comes right from the pit of Hell where I reside.

The first is the prevalence of polls in your society and news media. No more is there discussion about what is objectively right or wrong, and instead a poll is immediately taken to see what the public thinks. And since human nature is now basically good, and you are your own gods, what a majority of you thinks is now automatically good and proper!

Your culture has even reached the point where the poll results themselves are now the story. There is no more transcendent standard, only the latest opinions which become the new standard. And those standards can change on a dime, which creates moral chaos.

The second is more anecdotal. I was watching one of your cable news networks one day because they were going to have a very popular pastor on for an interview. I wanted to make sure the gotcha questions we had prepared for our proxy who was hosting the program would be asked. The first gotcha question was intended to be open-ended, in order to lead this celebrity pastor down the primrose path to viral embarrassment.

"Why do you believe in Christianity?" our guy hosting the program asked.

Without even a moment's hesitation this celebrity pastor blurted out, "Because it works for me."

We immediately spoke into the conscience of our proxy host to let that answer stand and not ask any follow-up questions, because this celebrity pastor had just articulated our utilitarian ethic without our prompting. This celebrity pastor was no danger to us but instead was an asset, so there was no reason to attempt anything that might risk his standing before the public. Quite the contrary, we've made sure to reward him with even more book deals, speaking engagements, and adoring fans.

See, if the standard is simply Christianity is true because it works for you that basically means *anything* that works for you can be true. Which means there is nothing that is transcendently true or false for all peoples in all places and at all times. Truth becomes subjective, not objective.

If that is your basis for believing in Christianity, you can have it and we will not meddle, because that is *not* Christianity.

Christianity is different than all the other religions of this world, most of which we've inspired or outright created. Every other religious system is based on creeds or a set of various "dos" and "don'ts," made up of burdens that must be met, because burdening your kind is one of our specialties.

But Christianity is based on the authenticity of a historical fact—did our dear old dad personally intervene in human history to raise the carpenter from the dead or not? Again, we take no official position on the matter down here, but that's beside the point.

The real point is Christianity flat out says it's not true if that whole resurrection thing didn't happen. That dreadful book explicitly says "if Christ has not been raised your faith is futile and you are still dead in your sins." Christianity leaves no room for middle ground here. It simply says if the carpenter is still dead, carry on with the rest of your lives, come what may, and his sincerest followers are the biggest dolts of all time. But if the tomb is empty, that changes everything and the world will never be the same.

There is nothing in there about one person getting to believe the resurrection is true and someone else does not, and they're both equally right and righteous. For how can two people have completely opposite beliefs regarding the most important existential fact in history, and still claim what they each believe to be simultaneously true? My, you bags of meat really are more gullible than I give you credit for.

It appears I will have to spell it out for you. Your culture is so screwed that you're now taking epistemological lessons from a demon like me. Stop and think about that for a second. Wait, now that I think about it, you probably don't even know what "epistemological" means, do you? Proving my point.

Something isn't true because it works, meat bags. Rather something works *because* it's true. For example, if someone decided that gravity didn't work for them and flung themselves off the top of a skyscraper without a parachute, would they land safely? No, their innards would be dispensed in glorious fashion throughout the below pavement. That's because gravity is an objective, transcendent truth. It preexists you and will outlive you. You don't get to change it, either, but you have to change for it or risk suffering the consequences.

After a while, even a lost culture figures out you can't exist very long without any objective truth. This brings us to the next phase—*everything* is true.

Stage 6—Syncretism

This is the blending of two or more belief systems into an already existing system, or with the intent of creating an entirely new one, that is necessary for building consensus within a culture.

Some examples might be "interfaith alliances," which call for various religions to set aside what makes them distinct in order to serve the common good (as if bad people would even know what the common good is). This is otherwise known as "social justice." Otherwise known as a complete and total scam.

Of course, you can't have justice in a society until you first deal with the unjust nature at the heart of the human condition, but you don't believe that anymore thanks to us. So you'll just keep trying to clean the outside of the cup instead.

One of my favorite examples are those "coexist" bumper stickers with the various religious symbols, because it says it so plainly and simply. As if it's so easy for people who have deep divisions over why they're on this planet, who put them there, and where history is ultimately heading to agree to disagree on such matters like they would their favorite sports team. Even funnier, the idiots buying this dime store logic think they're the most profound of you all!

You mean setting aside your differences is all you had to do all this time? Shucks, Sherlock, how come nobody ever previously thought of that?

One of the wittiest atheists of your era, who's being perpetually tormented down here with us now, exchanged letters with one of these syncretistic simpletons toward the end of his time on earth. This woman claimed to be "a liberal and tolerant Christian" who shared her disdain for those awful "fundamentalists," who arrogantly believe the words of that dreadful book are the ultimate truth.

She said that while living for Jee-zus works for her, there are many paths to "you know who," and she couldn't condemn someone who found another way that worked for them. She thought this famous atheist would respond to her "tolerance" approvingly.

She thought wrong.

This famous atheist wrote her back, and told her that if she didn't believe in things like the virgin birth and the literal physical resurrection of the carpenter, she wasn't much of a Christian at all. Nor did he have any respect for her softheaded rambling. He absolutely nuked her.

I actually had this exchange matted and framed for my Master's private office here in Hell, as a trophy of just how close I was to accomplishing my mission of taking you down. The atheists who believe in nothing are now explaining belief to the believer! My, how things have changed, but it wasn't always this way.

It used to be Christians or those influenced by Christianity composed Western Civilization's greatest music.

It used to be Christians or those influenced by Christianity created Western Civilization's greatest art.

It used to be that Christianity was the basis for Western Civilization's economic system you (used to) know as capitalism.

It used to be that dreadful book was the basis for moral truth in Western Civilization.

It used to be the greatest scientists were Christians who wanted to see evidence of "you know who's" handiwork in the natural world.

It used to be nearly all of the greatest universities in America were founded by believers for the purposes of discipling this nation.

Emphasis on the phrase *used to be*.

But what happens now is virtually every vestige of cultural rot and humanistic psychobabble Hell's most wicked minds can conjure up is welcomed within your halls of power, and the very moral and philosophical foundations of your Western Civilization and United States of America sleep with the fishes.

The cherry on top is how this has infested the various movements and institutions that should be opposing us as well.

Your "conservatives" and "evangelicals" pride themselves on being people of principle and virtue, but they are usually among the first to bow the knee to cultural acceptance. They are among the first who will throw their own overboard for saying something controversially true, all because it might hurt the overall movement. Translation: our opponents might call us bad names.

They are among the first to scorn the ones who do step out on principle and demand more integrity, referring to them spitefully as "purists." Correct me if I'm wrong, but doesn't that dreadful book numerous times call upon believers to be pure, abstain from that which is evil, and to be "holy" (or set apart from the world)?

Your conservative movement takes its most principled candidates in primaries and throws them under the bus, viewing them to be "unelectable." As if it's worth winning an election with a candidate who doesn't believe as you do in the first place. Rest assured, though, that later on that same movement will wring its hands about another political sellout—once the "electable" hack they helped win gets into office and proceeds to betray them on every front.

Your churches are even worse, because they should know better. Yet even there you've replaced elders with "boards of directors." You've replaced doctrine with "mission statements." You've replaced discipleship with programs. This is the language of marketing and corporations, not of a "city on a hill." Too many of your ministers are more concerned about building their own empire than they are prevailing against the gates of Hell. And we are prevailing upon them as a result.

All too often your churches have become so "relevant" they've actually become "relative." Meaning no one can tell the difference between them and the culture, and it's not because you're influencing the culture. It's because the culture is influencing you.

You might counter with "we have the most megachurches ever" or "we're selling more Christian merchandise than ever before." However, you are confusing "audience" with "influence." Those things are not always one and the same.

Some troubled boy who can shave might lead the world in Twitter followers, which is a big audience. But he's not negotiating Middle East peace accords, nor is he inventing a new technology or vaccine, which is how one gains influence. The person with the audience is hot now, but will soon be replaced with the next "hot now." The person with the influence leaves a legacy, no matter how troubled they may have been in life, which in its own way is immortality.

Just ask Edgar Allan Poe, who was considered a drunken loser most of his time on earth. Now he is recognized as one of the greatest writers your civilization has ever produced. Or a boxer like Joe Louis, who is one of the few among your species who can honestly say he was the greatest in the world at something that mattered to people, but died broken and busted. You don't remember the Poe and Louis who lost the battle with their own demons. Instead, since they were men of influence you remember them according to their legacy.

On the other hand, the pop culture sensation with the audience is usually not remembered at all. Or at least until VH1 takes us behind the music, where we'll find these former flashes in the pan now shaking their money maker for drunken cougars at the Whiskey-Tango-Foxtrot County Fair.

See, you've got a lot of Christian celebrities with an audience. Huge audiences, in fact. On the surface there's nothing wrong with having a huge audience. There was one particularly bothersome English pastor a couple of centuries ago who helmed a huge church in London. We did our best to vex him with bouts of depression and the like, but he rose above it to leave a legacy of preaching and teaching I still find repulsive today. Plus, let's face it: no one has a larger audience than the carpenter.

Except for my Master.

It's not having a large audience that is the problem for you, but rather how that audience was acquired. Do you acquire that audience by catering to their most carnal desires—sex, wealth, success, etc.—or by influencing them with something that will truly transform their lives?

Unfortunately for you, most of your churches with the largest audiences fail this test. Their methodology is the carrot and the stick, except it's all carrot and no stick. Everybody hears about "you know who's" love all the time, but you hardly ever hear about his wrath. Oh, despite the fact me and my fellow Hell spawn have you convinced his wrath isn't real, I can personally attest to the fact it is very real and very wrathful.

Hence the fact we're down here now.

That doesn't mean he doesn't love you, because he does. The fact you still exist at all after everything you've done to disobey him testifies to that fact. But he is not to be trifled with. He is the only one who can destroy the body and cast your eternal soul into Hell with us. He is still the most powerful being in the entire universe, though not as clever as my Master.

Yet you belong to us now, so we have you bags of meat convinced that if you just pretend our dear old dad isn't there, he's not. Lawd have mercy. Stop to consider how imbecilic you are. You literally think you can simply wish away a being that spoke you into existence, and with a snap of his finger can eliminate any record you ever existed.

Come to think of it, when I'm done with this book I'm going to ask my Master for a well-deserved raise. The further we get into this the more impressed with myself and what I've done to you I become.

Allow me to provide you a specific example of what it means for a Christian celebrity to have audience but no influence.

Let's begin with a pop quiz. If I told you a well-known Christian celebrity figure did the following:

- Repeatedly denied the main point of the carpenter's gospel
- Consistently watered down and distorted biblical teaching
- Believes the purpose of human life is to glorify yourself and not "you know who"

Which side would you say such a person is on?

A. Heaven
B. Hell

The Christian celebrity in question here is known as "America's Pastor." Pastor of what exactly is open to interpretation, depending on the prevailing winds of pop culture and what helps pad the bank account at the time.

We know you are visually and sensually driven creatures. So we like to appear to you, at least initially, as glamorous, titillating, and smiling with a bright double-decker of pearly whites. Never forget the most poisonous serpents are often the prettiest.

You fall for it because you judge based on what's on the outside, and from the outside America's pastor has it going on. He lives in a $10 million mansion with his movie star gorgeous wife. He's the rare plus-fifty man with six-pack abs. His publicity tours generate so much that demand scalpers can ask for up to $850 per ticket. He renovated an NBA team's old arena for over $100 million to house your nation's largest "church" there. His estimated net worth exceeds $40 million.

From the outside, America's pastor lives a life this world covets. There's just one problem with that. I can't think of a single truly great figure in the two-thousand-year history of Christianity who didn't pay some kind of worldly price for defending the teachings of the carpenter—beginning with the carpenter himself at the cross. However, it seems as if the world is paying him quite handsomely for the self-esteem gospel according to Joel.

By the way, while the cross where the carpenter allegedly died for the sins of the world is the most recognized symbol in history, you won't find one of those at America's pastor's "church." You won't find too much talk about suffering, sin, and salvation, either. Instead, you'll find a lot of shiny, happy people.

Just like America's pastor.

A team always takes on the characteristics of its (life) coach. After being beaten, imprisoned, shipwrecked, and beheaded for his beliefs, the wretch known as Paul who wrote most of the

New Testament would be unrecognizable to America's pastor's adherents.

Happiness draws an audience. You all want to be happy. The problem for you is what often makes you happy are the instruments of your destruction. For example, you do drugs to be happy, which is why you call it "getting high" and not "getting low."

But the carpenter sees what's on the inside. And what he sees is that something is very wrong with the inside of you. Your brains are broken. You're spiteful, greedy, selfish, dishonest, lustful, prideful, and at times capable of unspeakable evil—with just a little bit of prodding and encouragement from us.

You're not getting any better, either. Nowadays parents sue for "wrongful birth" because they didn't get the chance to kill their own kids before they were born, and moms publicly boast about "wishing every day" they could kill their children. The 20th century was the most technologically advanced, prosperous, and educated century in human history—and also the bloodiest.

Meanwhile, in America's pastor's hometown of Houston, the lesbian mayor he prayed a blessing over when she took office has been busy trying to intimidate the church into silencing its public witness. While his peers were being threatened with persecution, he was silent. But cut America's pastor some slack, he had his "A Night of Hope" events booked all over the country. Where hope comes every time the collection plate is passed, and paying customers get their hope first. It says so right there in the contract.

I wrote it myself.

So why wasn't America's pastor singled out for standing up to his pagan mayor's attempt to redefine morality in his city? When you learn the answer to that question, you'll know why he is so popular. A culture as toast as yours—drowning in its own selfishness, arrogance, and materialism—can't get enough of his forked tongue philosophy.

America's pastor isn't preaching the carpenter's gospel. He's preaching quicksand.

Quicksand, though, tickles the ears and draws an audience because you're telling people what they want to hear. It doesn't take any courage or conviction to preach quicksand, only cunning and ambition. Two traits we have in spades down here.

Influence, on the other hand, is countercultural. It swims against the tide, or creates a new one. Which explains why we have very few of your Christian celebrities on our hit list down here. Yes, there are certainly some drawing big crowds who are making our job more difficult, who correctly mix their prophetic witness and shrewd presentation without corrupting their calling.

No, I won't name them because I want the confusion in your ranks to remain.

However, I will tell you some of those we're the most afraid of are the unassuming ones. The ones who pour their life's work into the lives of the people in their congregations, with no expectation of worldly recognition. The ones who have no bells and whistles, but only the words of the carpenter to offer the world. Next to the words of that dreadful book, the local church is still the most devastating weapon the carpenter has at his disposal when it has such a humble and faithful leader.

Thankfully, your culture is in short supply of such men, and producing even less of them in the generation to come. All because those type of men draw clear lines between right and wrong, truth and error, good and evil. In your syncretistic culture you no longer desire that. So after these men die off they'll be replaced by ones who resemble Joel Osteen more so than Billy Graham.

Such a culture is now prepared for its final stage of decay.

Stage 7—Secular Humanism

This final stage is both a culture's death and rebirth.

The human will has a great desire to worship something. That "g-d–shaped hole in the heart" you may have read about. When a culture devolves into secular humanism, it's really just setting the stage for what will happen next. Revival is just around the corner; it's just a matter of what the source of the reviving is.

Secular humanism, or the belief in and worship of self above all, is best explained by the following fifteen points that originated from the deep recesses of my bowels. Currently some of your most useful idiots are promoting this tripe I literally pulled out of my own backside as enlightened thinking. So yes, your species literally has (my) feces for brains.

The universe wasn't created but just kind of happened. Like ya'll won the ultimate lottery or something. Of course, no one really knows when, how, or (most importantly) why it happened. But secular humanists claim to have all the answers nonetheless.

Mankind is not created in the image of "you know who" specially, but is one with and emerged alongside nature as part of purely materialistic processes – for which we don't know the origins or reasons obviously.

Human beings are not mind, body, and spirit but simply organic life. And no, it doesn't matter that you have cognitive ability far beyond any other organic life. Nor does that cognitive ability require any explanation for why you have it.

Mankind has only created culture and religion not because they're needs fundamental to the way you were made, but because of interaction with your natural environment and social heritage. In other words you're simply products of your environment.

On one hand secular humanism asserts there's all kinds of undiscovered "truths" out there just waiting to be known. On the other hand, any supernatural or cosmic claims to human worth, origin, and purpose must be rejected right away. There must be limits to our open-mindedness, don't you know.

Any belief system that adheres to moral absolutes, faith, or theism must be rejected as antiquated. Just because we said so.

There is no distinction between the sacred and the secular, but anything that purports to be founded in something higher than the human condition (which, of course, secular humanists get to decide what that means) is baseless. Some of you may wonder how secular humanists can simultaneously claim to be one with nature, while also claiming the preeminence of humanity. To which we say "shut up, bigots!"

The full focus of the secular humanist is on self-actualization in the here and now, for there is no afterlife. Thus, it's not about the destination but the journey. You still haven't found what you're looking for. You're spiritual but not religious. Blah, blah, blah…

Instead of superstitious worship or prayer, the secular humanist prioritizes social justice and self-esteem.

There is no need for religious connotations associated with anything supernatural. Anything occurring outside the natural world has a natural explanation. We just haven't found it yet, but we're so open minded we're confident we will. If our brains don't fall out first, that is.

We assume secular humanism will encourage what's best and healthy for the individual as well as the society as a whole with enough education. Now, we have absolutely no evidence in all of human history to make such a grand assumption. But you religionists are still sentimentalists at best, hate-mongers at worst – so there!

Religion may be tolerated so long as it encourages human achievement, which is another way of saying it will be tolerated so long as it ceases to be eternally significant whatsoever.

All worthy human institutions (and we decide what "worthy" is) have equal station and authority when it comes to determining human fulfillment. No religious institution or ecclesiastical methodology can claim preeminence over human affairs. And rest assured any that says otherwise will be called every name in the book, bullied to silence, and then driven underground if need be. Because, tolerance.

Secular humanists believe profit-motive is a bad thing (unless we're the ones doing the profiting). In its place, a socialized economic order must be established for the purposes of redistribution of wealth and "income equality." Of course, such terms are never clearly defined on purpose, so they can be used to justify punishing what we oppose and promoting what we favor as we see fit.

We assert that secular humanism will affirm life by denying its ultimate origin and purpose. And even establish satisfactory life for all by benefiting just a few (namely those of us who know how you should live your life better than you do). Oh, and rules and regulations demanding compliance and good morale will be strictly enforced at all times.

Two things should stand out about what you just read.

First, for all the high-minded and enlightened talk, what's articulated here has ushered in perhaps the most brutal and barbaric era in your species' history. For which my Master is quite proud of me.

Second, this is the culmination of everything you've read in this book up until this point. Which means your civilization is not sustainable. It is infested with termites, unseen to the naked eye, but inside the walls are decaying the foundation as we speak.

As you systematically carry out the fifteen points of our manifesto, you will commit what amounts to societal suicide—destroying the very institutions, traditions, and systems your forefathers established to stop me from doing this to you in the first place. You've basically implanted the virus that is erasing your own hard drive.

Then, once the system reboots, your so-called "American Exceptionalism" will be lost forever. Fret not, though, for it will be replaced by something else. I haven't quite made up my mind for sure what that will be yet, and certainly my Master must sign off on any final decision, but I'm leaning heavily toward recommending *Allahu Akbar* at the moment.

So you might want to consider brushing up on your Arabic. Just in case.

CHAPTER 7

Despair

We have now reached the tipping point moment for a culture in
deep doo-doo like your own. When your collapse is so imminent
and anticipated you create what amounts to a self-fulfilling
prophecy. Instead of us aiding and abetting you, you're aiding
and abetting us.

Apocalypse is much on your mind these days. So many of
your movies, books, and television shows feature apocalyptic
themes. Even your children play apocalyptic video games that
just recycle the killing over and over again, with no redemption
or victory in sight.

Hope is in short supply in America these days.

A few months before this book was completed, an all-time
record low of only 13 percent of Americans thought the country
was on the right track. Another poll found Americans ranked
your own government as your country's biggest problem four
months in a row.

But for the clearest picture yet of the rampant despair in your culture, check out these results from the 2014 General Social Survey:

Overall confidence in government is at record lows.

Only 23 percent of Americans have confidence in the Supreme Court, 11 percent in the presidency, and only 5 percent in Congress.

Regardless of having a Democrat in the White House, Democrats' confidence in the executive branch has plummeted to just 18 percent. Regardless of having a Republican-controlled Congress, only 3 percent of Republicans have confidence in the legislative branch.

Despite all this angst, 91 percent of incumbents were reelected in 2012, and your 2014 election saw the lowest voter turnout since World War II. Those numbers tell me you've all but given up. Unlike Howard Beale, you're mad as Hell but you're going to keep taking it anyway.

Despair is in the air, and it's music to my ears.

Recently, a progressive group called Campaign for America's Future listed "Seven Signs That the American Dream is Dying":

Most people can't get ahead financially. They noted your middle class hasn't seen its wages increase in fifteen years.

The stay-at-home parent is a thing of the past. The money line here was "having a child is now the single best predictor that a woman will end up in a financial collapse."

Student debt is crushing a generation of non-wealthy Americans. College costs have risen 500 percent since 1985.

Vacations aren't for the likes of you anymore. They cited an American Express study that found the average vacation for a family of four costs $4,720.

Even with health insurance, medical care is increasingly unaffordable for most people. Health care costs are increasing at a rate of 8 percent per year for the average American household, while median household income has fallen by at least 8 percent.

Americans no longer look forward to a secure retirement. The United States ranks only nineteenth among industrialized countries when it comes to retirement security.

The rich are more debt-free, while others have no choice. They say, "American households have become dependent on debt to maintain their standard of living in the face of stagnant wages."

Set aside for a second, hard as that may be, how the very progressive policies that come from our playbook is one of the primary reasons for these troubling signs in the first place (you're welcome, by the way). I mean the one percent it's decrying voted for the progressive candidate for president in 2008 and 2012. Nevertheless, this organization still stumbled upon the truth, even if they're ignorant of the cause.

Every aspect of the American Dream previous generations took for granted is eroding for this one, which explains why 76 percent of Americans told the *Wall Street Journal* they no longer believe their children's generation will be better off than they were.

And you know what? They're right.

Millennials have already become the first generation in US history to see a decline in their standard of living, and that's before the full entitlements bill for the massive baby boom generation arrives.

The cloud of despair hovering over your culture even touches personal relationships. According to *The Huffington Post*, a record high two-thirds of Americans say you can't trust people. Healthline says the number of patients diagnosed with depression increases by approximately 20 percent each year. (I'm hoping some of you will become depressed while reading this, as a matter of fact.) And the states with the highest rates of depression are—get this—West Virginia, Oklahoma, Tennessee, Arkansas, Louisiana, Mississippi, and Alabama. All places right in the buckle of the "Bible Belt." So not even Jee-zus can pull you out of your funk, it seems.

That's enough to make even this surly demon crack a smile.

Despite turning "diversity" into a quasi-religion, yours is a culture as balkanized as ever. Only 15 percent of Americans believe race relations have improved since the election of your country's first black president. "Race pimps" (those who foment racial strife because it's good for their bank accounts) are all the rage. They even get their own prime time television shows. These so-called "ministers" are really just shameless opportunists. Trust me, I would know and let's just leave it at that.

Come on, what kind of ministers have children out of wedlock and are tax cheats? Why, the kind we recruit, of course.

All this race-baiting is having a boomerang effect that showed up in your 2014 elections. The crucial swing state of Ohio went for a black presidential candidate twice in 2008 and 2012, but the Democratic candidate for governor there only received 24 percent of the white vote in 2014. Obama had received 41 percent of the white vote just two years prior.

Look at the way some in your media immediately rush to judgment in racially charged incidents like the shooting death of Michael Brown in Ferguson, Missouri. An entire "hands up, don't shoot" meme was created that went viral nationwide. The officer who shot Brown, Darren Wilson, was all but convicted of being a racist cop in the court of public opinion. The city was plunged into persistent rioting.

However, by the time it was all said and done, even your race-baiting Justice Department had to admit it was all a lie, including the "hands up, don't shoot" part. Furthermore, it turned out Wilson was right to shoot Brown, who was basically a thug.

So if you're keeping score at home, one of the more successful middle-class black communities in your country was decimated by riots driven by a false racial narrative, which accomplished nothing other than destroying private property and jobs that largely belonged to blacks. Because nothing says "social justice" like looting the local Quickie Mart for a pack of menthols and some Ding Dongs.

Look, like I keep telling you, I'm a demon (and a damned good one). I'm an agent of chaos. I enjoy watching your destruction. I get off on it actually. I completely and totally hate you with every fiber of my being. I have a very dim view of your species' prospects. Nevertheless, even I have never seen a people so far gone they destroy their own infrastructure in an effort to get back at their alleged oppressors.

I mean, shouldn't you be destroying "the man's" property instead of your own? What exactly do you think you're proving by burning down your own homes and businesses? Did the French burn down their own villages to protest the oppression of the aristocracy? No, they stormed the Bastille.

Lawd, you can't even riot right.

Even worse, recent riots in Baltimore are another prime example. Set aside for a moment the fact the person whose death sparked the unrest had been arrested *eighteen times*. The protesting thugs and morons who rioted did more damage to their own neighborhoods than the man allegedly keeping them down ever could. This is pointless debauchery. Utter lawlessness.

There's no meaning here, other than a culture off the rails.

These are boys who can shave that needed a daddy to spank them a long time ago. This isn't "no justice, no peace." This is the blind leading the blind.

Here's a novel idea: Go to class. Get a job . . . oh wait, you can't, because you keep voting for people and policies that have dumped vats of turds on your schools, destroyed your families, incentivized immorality, given all the entry-level jobs needed to start your way up the workforce to illegal aliens for dirt wages, and empowered the very government outfitting cops to look like they're ready to invade Iran.

By golly, who's surprised that didn't work out? I know I'm not, since I planned the whole thing myself!

There's no entrepreneurship creating new jobs, because no one wants to go places where they'll be taxed to death or assaulted. In short, this is the culmination of operating outside of those natural laws we previously spoke of for far too long. You create a vicious cycle, by which you need government to keep the lights on, but then the taxpayers required to keep government's lights on flee to greener and safer pastures.

So government has to acquire more and more power, and do so by incentivizing more and more self-destruction to acquire more and more victims to justify its growth. Then you're shocked when tensions of so many lost people boil over, and are shocked again when the very government that created this mess isn't equipped to clean it up.

The despair caused by your racial strife also means you're far less likely to tackle real and substantive issues of racial injustice in your culture. On one hand, the race pimps won't touch those issues with a 10,000-foot pole, because they can't polarize them enough to make them profitable. But then most whites become so jaundiced by the playing of the "race card" whatsoever they automatically tune them out on the other.

The black unemployment rate has been a major problem pretty much since the advent of the welfare state (no coincidence by the way), but now it's higher than the unemployment rate was during the Great Depression. The National Urban League says the average individual net worth (income/assets minus debt, for those of you who went to public school) of blacks is a meager $6,000 compared to $110,500 for whites. The National Urban League also notes San Francisco, which it calls itself the "bastion of progressive politics," ranked dead last out of seventy major metropolitan areas in median income equality.

Even though your FBI combines Hispanics with Caucasians as "whites" in its statistical reporting, the crime numbers are still staggering. A white homicide victim is more than twice as likely to be killed by a black than a black is to be killed by a white. The number one cause of death for young black men between the ages of 15 and 24 is homicide, with 93 percent of those murders committed by other blacks. Forty-nine percent of black males are arrested before their twenty-third birthday. A recent study of inmates in North Carolina found that black men were safer behind bars than living free outside prison walls. Blacks are about 13 percent of the total population, but are almost half of the nation's prison population.

Then there's education.

About 50 percent of blacks graduate from high school, while more than 75 percent of whites do. Black kids K–12 are more than twice as likely to be suspended from school. On average, a black twelfth-grade student reads at the level of a white eighth-grade student. Only 14 percent of black eighth graders score at a proficient level. A black college dropout has the same chances of getting a job as a white high school dropout. Black college graduates are twice as likely to be unemployed as other college graduates. Only about 40 percent of blacks who enroll in a four-year college will graduate from one.

Yet most of you reading this don't know nearly as much about these social problems as you do that time Don Imus referred to the Rutgers University women's basketball team as "nappy-headed hos."

Which reminds me, would you like to know which state led the nation in black graduation rate? Why Texas, the ultimate "red state" did, graduating 84 percent of its black students despite ranking in the bottom third nationally in money spent per pupil. That's more than twenty points better than progressive nirvana New York, which also spends twice as much money per pupil as Texas does.

Which only goes to show our "just throw other people's money at it" propaganda is total bunk, but thank you for swallowing it hook, line, and sinker nonetheless.

Want more despair? How about the battle of the sexes?

Breitbart News, one of the leading conservative news outlets, ran a two-part series in 2014 called "The Sexodus." It laid out in great detail how young men are giving up on women. They believe young women don't know what they want, that they as men can't win either way, and with the proliferation of pornography they don't need to put up with real women in order to achieve the gratification they crave.

You can find the exact same kind of articles from the women's perspective as well without looking too hard. In fact, a Google search for "women giving up on marriage" returned over 111 *million* hits ("men giving up on marriage" returned "only" 41 million).

Recently, an Ivy League–educated mother of two enraged feminists (which admittedly doesn't take much) when she wrote an open letter to the *Daily Princetonian* urging the girls at her alma mater to find a husband before they leave school. Her argument seemed rational enough: "You will never again be surrounded by this concentration of men who would be worthy of you."

But when you've done a number on a culture like I have on you, there is no place for rational. Only the emotional. The article generated a hundred million hits according to the *New York Daily News*, including lots from feminists angry at the mere suggestion a woman might need a man.

I think I might've posted a few of those comments myself, if I remember right. Or it might have been one of my associates. We've got a whole brigade of grunt demons down here whose full-time work is devoted to trolling the comments sections of every important news/philosophy/pop culture/theology website. Our goal is to discourage you into thinking you're the only one who still believes in anything traditional and wholesome if you read them. They usually pose as the most rabid and irrational homosexual activists, but they pull off man-hating feminist really well, too.

But enough with data and other anecdotal sources, let's get down to the real reason why your culture is irrevocably awash in despair.

To put it bluntly, look in the mirror.

The aforementioned G. K. Chesterton was once asked to respond to a newspaper that was posing the question, "What's wrong with the world?"

Chesterton famously responded with a one-word answer: "Me."

You are what is wrong with this awful place. Hell would be bleak enough, but the fact we have to spend eternity here with so many of you makes it even worse. Oh, sure, the screams and cries of torment that go on constantly down here, and are so loud you can hardly hear yourself think half the time, make it sound like you're getting the raw end of the deal. But it's really the other way around.

Let me let you in on a dirty little secret. We don't have to torture you down here. *We choose to. We want to. Because we hate you.*

We're here in this place of despair because of you. Because our dear old dad chose to love you more than he loved us. It is not in his nature to sadistically torture the beings he created. Hell, we openly rebelled against him and the worst he did to us was to banish us from his presence forever (or until my Master convinces him he was wrong).

You'd be tormented enough to learn there really is a benevolent, all-powerful being who built a place in paradise just for you. But you were too stupid to take him up on it, and will now live without your deepest need being filled for all of eternity as a result. Imagine the anguish your soul will feel knowing what you always wanted was right there waiting for you, but you took a pass.

For your soul, that is worse than corporal or even capital punishment. That is solitary confinement with no possibility of parole. Annihilation is preferable to that type of isolation. After a while you'd be begging to be put out of your misery rather than continuing to contemplate your fate.

Isolation from your primary reason for being is awful, yes, but it's nothing compared to what we do to you. And no, it's not for your own good. This isn't like your daddy taking you over his knee to teach you a lesson. This is unspeakable masochism not even a warped mind like Clive Barker can adequately articulate.

If I pulled no punches in sharing with you exactly what my peers and I are prepared to do to you once you arrive, I couldn't get this book published anywhere except on the black market. I'd end up on a terrorist watch list. You'd probably puke just reading it. Imagine your worst, most craven way to inflict pain on your worst enemy, and multiply it by infinity.

That's just an average day in Hell.

Of course, I am aware of prophecies that claim we will all burn in the "lake of fire" one day for what we're doing, but I am confident my Master will convince "you know who" how wrong he is about you before that were to happen. I have literally bet my life on my Master, and he hasn't let me down yet.

But what have you bet your life on? Thanks to my genius plan you've basically bet on your sorry selves.

That's a bad bet, because you're bad. Your nature is fallen. You're not basically good. So imagine what happens when you get large groups of such fundamentally flawed people together in one community or culture, most of whom are largely relying on their own impulses, desires, and instincts to get what they want out of life.

Shared sacrifice is replaced by selfishness.

Honor is replaced by victimology.

Love is replaced by lust.

Commitment is replaced by cohabitation (and doesn't that sound hot).

Complementary is replaced by confrontation.

The "melting pot" is replaced by a hyphen.

There are really only two things your species has in common with one another. You're all made in the image of our dear old dad, and apart from him you're nothing but animals with cognitive reasoning.

How do they live in the animal kingdom? Well, like animals, you idiot. I find it hilarious when some make the argument for mainstreaming certain sexual practices because "they're found in nature." Except the flinging of one's feces, the feeding of your offspring with your own vomit, and the licking of one's own dung hole is found in nature, too. Perhaps you might want to aim a little higher than that?

Yet you can't. Because estranged from your creator, there's not much difference between you and the animal kingdom. You're just the top of the food chain, that's all. Capable of causing far worse devastation than even a great white shark or a hive of killer bees, because you can manipulate your environment to your advantage in ways they cannot. If a lion could just invent a gun to hunt antelope, he would and take out the whole herd at once, but he can't and is forced to hunt them one at a time. You, however, can invent such things—and much worse.

And you will keep on inventing such things, some terrific and some terrible, in the hopes of "making the world a better place." Unfortunately, when you reach the top of your Tower of Babel and realize it doesn't fulfill you as anticipated, you have a choice to make. Either humble yourselves and realize this world has nothing for you. Or eat, drink, and be merry, for tomorrow you die.

Most of you will choose unwisely, much to my glee, which means sooner than you realize we'll be choosing how to brutalize you once you arrive. Maybe you'll bring your whole family with you. Oh, yes, that is my absolute favorite style of torture.

To take the patriarch of a family and spare him the worst of it, but then make him watch while we do unimaginable things to the souls of his wife and offspring right there in front of him. We will tie him down so that he can't intercede on their behalf, and then bring the action so close to him he can literally feel the brunt of their heaves and cries.

This is for the man who chose not to lead his family down the right path in life. Like his father Adam, he stood passively by while we tempted them to go astray. He then made excuses while they succumbed, and never took the initiative to lead them back to the narrow road and fight for them.

Now, here in Hell, he suddenly does want to fight for them. But by then it's way too late. There are no second chances in Hell. This is where you end up when your chances run out.

My Master came up with the genius idea of blindfolding the family members, and then making them think it was their daddy committing these atrocities against them. So the daddy doesn't just have to watch what we're doing to the family he led right to our doorstep, but he has to listen to them curse him for it in the most brutal language as well.

That is perhaps the greatest feeling of failure possible for your species, and perhaps a foreshadowing of what's to come when our dear old dad finally admits his failure as your father and ends this ridiculous experiment called humanity.

Think of getting to eat your favorite foods every day the rest of your miserable life with no fear of getting fat. Then you'd know how much we delight in hearing the patriarch beg us to let him take the pain and anguish we inflict on his loved ones upon himself instead. But Hell is no place for sacrificial love. That's the carpenter's racket.

Hell is a place of despair. Just like America is becoming.

CHAPTER 8

Death

In every war there are moments that turn the tide.

In your Civil War it was Gettysburg. In World War II's Pacific theater it was the Battle of Midway. And in the war for the collective soul of your civilization, it was when you began to embrace and celebrate a culture of death.

All other debaucheries stem from no longer valuing life. This is the source of the river by which all other lakes and tributaries of cultural rot flow. For once you no longer value the most sacred gift of all—the gift of life—you will no longer value any lesser blessings as well. Once you devalue life, you detach yourselves from showing any restraint whatsoever.

When a culture becomes so self-loathing it no longer fights for its own survival, and incentivizes behaviors that hasten its extinction, that is a culture just playing out the string. Literally just lying there like a wounded animal, waiting for someone to come along and put it out of its collective misery.

That culture is you, and I volunteer myself for that job.

Your belief that life has no greater meaning other than the avoidance of suffering is why you're embracing death as deliverance. However, the carpenter lived specifically so he could suffer for you on your behalf. If it weren't for his suffering, much of which I played a direct hand in, none of your lives would have any meaning at all. All of you would be our cannon fodder, just waiting to expire up there before permanently perspiring down here. We'd be so overrun with your sorry souls there would be no more room at Hell's Inn.

But despite the fact you disobey our dear old dad every bit as much as we do, he has still prepared a place for you in his paradise. Through the carpenter you have a hope to change your much-deserved fate, and our only hope is to convince our dear old dad you are his great mistake. None of us are perfect, not even "you know who" despite that dreadful book's claims to the contrary.

The joke that is your species is living proof of that. We're all in need of a mulligan once in eternity, even him. We seek to prove to him you're so worthless you're not worth saving, and he shouldn't have made you in the first place.

Your enthusiasm for death is bolstering our case.

To exalt death is the ultimate middle finger to "you know who," because he is the author of all life. Literally nothing could or would exist without him. You would be less than nothing without him. The universe wouldn't have even conceived of you at all. His greatest gift to you is life, for it is required to experience any other blessings and fulfill any purpose. So to give up on the value of life makes you an ingrate. It's like wishing your earthly daddy had worn a condom on the night you were conceived.

The controversial sagas of two recent women best exemplify your dark embrace of a culture of death.

Brittany Maynard became a national cause célèbre when she was profiled in *People* for wanting to "die on my own terms." Diagnosed with stage four brain cancer, Maynard was given six months to live.

Since it's "a terrible way to die" (her words), Maynard convinced her family to move her to Oregon, where she could take advantage of the state's euthanasia laws. Maynard even spent some of her last remaining moments on earth urging other states to adopt so-called "death with dignity" laws.

Except there's no such thing as a dignified death. I know, because perhaps no one other than "you know who" and my Master has seen more of your species die than have I.

Death in and of itself is an indignity, and only by recognizing this do you *Homo sapiens* truly understand the meaning of life. For instance, Maynard bragged about climbing Mount Kilimanjaro before she got sick. Yet if life is only about avoiding suffering, why did Maynard risk her life to make such a climb?

Falling off Mount Kilimanjaro doesn't exactly tickle. It's also in one of the most remote parts of this planet, so you could fall and be lost there for who knows how long. That's also a "terrible way to die." Three things can happen when you try to climb Mount Kilimanjaro, and two of them are bad.

Seeking that dignified death, Maynard eventually ended her own life with the help of a physician. So much for that Hippocratic oath. For thousands of years the taking of one's own life has been commonly referred to as "suicide." Nowadays we've so muddied your moral waters that even suicide is a postmodern construct. Thus, Maynard maintained until the end she was not committing suicide by committing suicide.

Maynard was elevated to hero status by many in your culture, and congratulated for her "courage." Funny, this demon is old enough to remember when you meat bags considered suicide to be a coward's way out. Yet now you so devalue life you consider it brave to put yourselves down like a rabid dog.

"There is not a cell in my body that is suicidal or wants to die," Maynard told *People*. "I want to live. I wish there was a cure for my disease but there is not."

What Maynard was seeking—the dignified death—cannot be found. Death is only in this world because the indignity of your sin brought that curse upon yourselves. You were originally created to live with our dear old dad forever, but you sided with my Master instead—and he brings carnage and chaos with him wherever he goes.

Death is the result of the suffering you bags of meat have caused this world, not some idle occurrence that is merely the natural way of things. This is why the wretched Jew named Paul wrote the carpenter "conquered the last enemy" death when he allegedly rose from the grave (again, our official position is to neither confirm nor deny that actually happened).

There is no death, indignity, or suffering to fear once you acknowledge the death and suffering the carpenter endured on your behalf. You used to know this. There once was a day, not too long ago, when virtually every American knew John 3:16.

"For g-d so loved the world that he gave his only son, that whosoever believes in him will not perish, but have eternal life."

However, after getting worked over by me, most Americans' favorite bible verse is now Matthew 7:1, completely taken out of context, of course. You only know the "judge not lest ye be judged" part, but virtually nothing the carpenter said before and after that. You just know to play that as your get out of jail free card the minute someone tries telling you what you're doing is wrong.

You only know that because you don't want to know the rest. You want to perish almost as much as we want to destroy you.

You not only don't believe in eternal life anymore, but you seek death. Remember when the story of a limited time to live meant going out with a bang, making your way through your bucket list, or giving inspiring speeches to those you'll leave behind to make sure they make every moment count?

While there is no such thing as a dignified death, there is such a thing as a meaningful death. How, why, where, or when someone dies can testify to the meaning (worth/dignity) of that person's life. This is why that dreadful book commemorates sacrificial love, because there is no greater love than a willingness to give one's life for another. You can give no more than your own self.

On the other hand, we demons would never sacrifice ourselves for one another. If anything, we frequently have to work separately and not in large groups because mo' demons means mo' problems. If you get too much evil concentrated in one place, zany hijinks will always ensue. Now, I would lay down my life for my Master, as would the rest of my demonic brethren, but that is not motivated by sacrificial love.

It is motivated by allegiance.

There is none of what you call "love" outside of the providence of "you know who," for he is love incarnate. Therefore, you cannot "love" something or someone outside of the will of the being who is solely responsible for love's meaning and existence. What you often call "love"—your sexual depravity, your materialism, your idolatry, etc.—is really your "allegiance" to your sin. Your sin being your master.

You have literally chosen your rebellion from "you know who" over his love—just like we have down here in Hell. In case you haven't figured this out by now, we have a lot more in common than you previously thought. We don't make you choose rebellion, you do that of your own free will, but we do play a part in convincing you to call your rebellion "love."

For the more you falsely love your sin, the less you will realize your need for the only true love in this universe. Again, my Master's masterful handiwork.

Back to Maynard. By making the decision to end her own life, Maynard assumed she had nothing more to offer this world or her loved ones beyond that point. That is to say in essence she was playing god and making decisions as if she alone knew the future.

How did she know a loved one wasn't going to need a comforting word from her the day after she took her life? How did she know her husband might not need her support for a major ordeal or trial two or three days later? How did she know she wasn't intended to be the one that was going to play a key part in saving someone's life a week later? How did she know a miraculous cure wouldn't be discovered two weeks later?

Boy, that would suck, wouldn't it? You're convinced there's no hope so you decide to "die with dignity," and then just weeks after they put you in the ground they find a cure. Could you imagine that?

I most certainly can, but I have a pretty twisted sense of humor.

Chances are if you take your own life you're probably going to end up down here with us, because most of the people that truly understand life is a gift from "you know who" wouldn't squander it like that. So imagine you're down here being tormented indescribably after taking your own life, but a cure was found for your disease so you didn't have to. Evilness, you talking monkeys are a laugh a minute.

People described Maynard as "fearless," but ironically it seems as if her decision to commit suicide was based solely out of fear. The fear of physical suffering. The fear of how it will negatively impact her loved ones. The fear of becoming undignified as a result of a terrible affliction.

Before you judge Maynard too harshly, realize these are all fears most of you don't understand, but I know someone who does—my Master.

My Master revels in fear. He is fear incarnate. If faith is the currency of heaven, then fear is the currency of Hell. Whenever you make fear-based decisions you are fueling the pit of Hell, for fear moves my Master to act the same way your faithful prayer moves "you know who."

Another woman's story also proves the tide has been turned.

An attractive Florida girl once decided she needed to go on a diet. When she didn't get enough potassium in her system, she passed out on the floor, eventually slipping into a coma. Her name was Terri Schiavo.

Although doctors said she would likely never fully recover from her dieting accident, Schiavo eventually improved to stable condition. She could even smile and react to her parents, which she does in the final video her parents took of her before she died. A video that you can easily find and watch for yourself online. Nevertheless, authorities denied her water and starved her to death in broad daylight in a Florida nursing home.

It was "the compassionate thing to do" after all! I think I speak for all of Hell when I say we agree!

The state of Florida also decided it was "the compassionate thing to do" to post armed guards outside of Schiavo's nursing home door, lest anyone sneak in and feed her ice chips so that she wouldn't starve to death.

This actually happened, just as I told you, in your country just a few years ago. This isn't a story from some totalitarian regime in your history books, or even from some "progressive" state that has embraced all of the craziness Hell has to offer. This happened in Florida, one of the most popular and picturesque states in your union.

Bobby Schindler was Schiavo's brother. In 2014 he wrote about the "culture of death" for a website called LifeNews:

It is estimated that 92 percent of all women who receive a prenatal diagnosis of Down Syndrome abort their baby. Currently, there is a strong push advocating the removal of spoon feeding from Alzheimer's patients if they so requested in an advance directive.

Sadly, these are just a few more recent examples of the life-threatening prejudices plaguing the disability community and countless other medically vulnerable. Indeed, this terrible toll does not arise in a cultural vacuum, but reflects attitudes that assume dead is better than disabled. It was not long ago that feeding tubes were considered basic and ordinary care and therefore it was illegal, an act of euthanasia, to stop feeding and hydrating a person in need of a feeding tube.

Today, however, feeding tubes have been redefined as "artificial nutrition and hydration"—and therefore a form of "medical treatment." Consequently, the removal of food and water from cognitively disabled patients, and countless other medically vulnerable, is now legal, and routine in all fifty states. Today, either the general public is unaware of this change, or they just don't care.

But if you think dehydrating to death our medically vulnerable isn't happening, then you are not paying attention. Whatever the reason, the mainstream media does very little to properly clear up any confusion that may exist, as they continue to report that persons who receive food and water via feeding tubes are receiving "artificial life support," giving the perception that these people are aided by machines.

Tragically, too many of us today have become disconnected and desensitized to our own dignity and intrinsic worth. It seems we no longer know how to love, and we place more significance and value on what a person can or cannot do, instead of understanding the value and dignity of the human person, simply because they are human.

As a consequence, every single day, decisions are being made for our medically defenseless to be barbarically starved and dehydrated to death. Not to mention the offensive claim that to slowly dehydrate persons to death over a period of weeks is an act of compassion; that they are somehow experiencing death in a dignified way.

This is not compassion, this is not love. This is intentionally killing, and in the most undignified way.

Everything Schindler says here is absolutely correct. And I can't tell you how happy I am to write that.

The stories of Maynard and Schiavo are living proof yours has become a culture of death. As is the fact your progressive politicians are fond of claiming they're being "my brother's keeper" by bankrupting your economy with a welfare state. Hilariously, they're quoting the first murderer in world history with that catchphrase. For this is what Cain said after he murdered his brother, Abel. Using the phrase to flippantly respond to our dear old dad when he questioned him about the whereabouts of his brother, who was killed by Cain's hands.

I know, because I was there, urging Cain on the whole way.

You are so enamored with death you celebrate the words of the world's first murderer in your political speak. But I won't stop there, because then I'd miss out on the opportunity to write about one of my personal favorites—Kermit Gosnell.

Many of you reading this probably have no idea who Gosnell is, despite the fact he's one of your country's most successful mass murderers, because much of your media did its best to bury his rampage. They were concerned telling the Gosnell story would reflect poorly on your abortion industry, and they view killing unborn children as a civic virtue. They're all-in for the culture of death. Some of them work directly for us.

Gosnell is serving a life sentence without parole in a Pennsylvania state prison after he was convicted of three counts of first-degree murder, one count of involuntary manslaughter, twenty-one felony counts for performing illegal abortions, and 211 counts of violating a state law that requires a woman to have "informed consent" before deciding to kill her baby.

Those charges may sound heinous to you, but they barely scratch the surface when it comes to describing Gosnell's seventeen-year macabre body of work. All of it taking place in his Philadelphia clinic, which was described as a "house of horrors" by the authorities who investigated him.

I have taken the liberty of preparing a summary of the most gruesome testimony from the Gosnell trial, just to give you a mere glimpse of his handiwork. While it pales in comparison to what many of you reading this will see down here one day, I can see the resemblance nevertheless.

Kareema Cross worked for Gosnell for a harrowing four years. Helping with child killing procedures in conditions so bad that she snapped photos to document them, and then reported her boss to the authorities under a fictitious name.

But nobody listened. Because, reproductive freedom and all.

Two years later, authorities raided Gosnell's clinic thinking it was a pill mill, only to discover that it was frighteningly so much more. In other words, they went in there for reasons totally unrelated to the babies Gosnell was butchering. Dismembering babies didn't move them to act, but the potential of Gosnell dealing prescription drugs under the table did. Who says your priorities are out of whack?

Cross said her training for working with Gosnell consisted of observing one ultrasound procedure and after that she was on her own. When Cross got a measurement of a baby in the womb beyond twenty-four weeks, she would have one of the other women who were better using the relic from the 1980s to verify her findings. The twenty-four weeks measurement was key, because it is illegal to abort an unborn child after twenty-three weeks and six days in Pennsylvania.

However, if the child is at twenty-two weeks, you can literally tear him apart limb from limb, rip the flesh of his puny little bones, and pay it no mind. I love this country!

If the child was beyond twenty-four weeks, Gosnell himself would always redo those ultrasounds. Gosnell was just going to make the ultrasound say whatever the law said it needed to say. If Pennsylvania banned killing unborn babies at sixteen weeks, Gosnell would manipulate the results to say that. If the ban was at thirty weeks, he was going to lie about that. And so on, and so forth. He's a killer of children. Why would anyone trust him to tell the truth?

Cross described in vivid detail her experiences at Gosnell's clinic. She testified that at first she began just taking vital signs and working the front desk. Duties as a medical assistant she was qualified to do. But after two weeks, Cross was asked to start doing ultrasounds, injecting drugs when Gosnell wasn't in the building, and assisting in the grungy, bloodstained procedure rooms.

While she worked for Gosnell, **Cross testified that at least twice a day, six days a week, at least two babies would be birthed before Gosnell ever arrived. She said an unlicensed medical school graduate, with a grisly curiosity about abortions, would be there to snip the babies' necks. She saw him do it at least fifty times!**

She saw this medical assistant take babies that were born alive (of course, they're already "alive" in their mother's womb), not stillborn but alive, and she saw this medical assistant murder at least fifty of them. When babies were born in Gosnell's presence, he would do the dirty deed himself.

Cross sometimes worked from 8:00 a.m. to 3:00 a.m. the next morning helping with procedures. Gosnell's clinic was a prolific killing machine that would've made any oppressive tyrant proud. Cross routinely saw babies born alive that were moving, breathing, and moaning. Cross held her hands about sixteen inches apart during her testimony to show how big those babies were.

Once in Gosnell's absence, Cross once saw a large baby delivered into a toilet. She saw his little arms and legs moving

in a swimming motion as he was trying to get out of the toilet. Gosnell severed the baby's neck to kill it right there in front of the mother, who was bleeding into the toilet. A nurse then placed the baby's remains in a container and whisked it away.

Let me pause right there for a second. I am a demon who hates your species with every fiber of my being, and takes joy in causing it great pain. Yet even I am disgusted at that. Pleased, for sure, to see your savagery confirmed, but disgusted nonetheless.

Now back to more mayhem.

Cross testified that another worker once called her over to see a baby that had just been born. Cross saw the baby's chest heaving up and down in steady breathing motions. The other nurse reached down and brought the hand up, but the newborn pulled it away on its own strength. **Cross said she saw the baby breathing for about twenty minutes on its own before the other nurse murdered the child by snapping its spinal cord with scissors.**

When the nurse who killed that child testified under oath at the Gosnell trial, she appeared emotionless and stared blankly ahead throughout. Almost as if she was in a catatonic state. Often taking uncomfortably long pauses. Instead of allowing herself to experience a deep, convicting guilt that might've led to repentance, she went the cognitive dissonance route.

Science!

Cross testified she observed self-breathing babies on more than ten occasions. Once she testified she even heard a whimpering cry. A fifteen-year-old girl was working in the killing room where that crying sound originated, and sought Cross's help with what to do. A teenage girl, perhaps one day destined to be a mother herself, was being trained how to kill children instead of raising them.

Progress!

Pretty much everyone that worked for Gosnell administered medications without supervision, even though none were qualified to do so. Several of the ladies tried to follow the mixing charts when administering sedation, but Cross noticed two nurses did not follow proper procedures while drugging women. On occasion, some receiving those injections complained to Cross about their swollen arms. Cross complained about their way of handling the drugs to Gosnell, but nothing changed.

Fed up with the conditions and the appalling way women were treated at Gosnell's clinic (besides the little women Cross helped Gosnell kill), Cross began to document the horrific conditions with her own camera. The full-color pictures were shown to a darkened courtroom on a large viewing screen. She photographed the blood-soaked procedure table in the operating room, which had rips in the vinyl where women laid during their abortions. The same table had been seized from the clinic and was present in the courtroom throughout the prosecution's case. **Some of the rust on the table was actually described as dried blood.**

But wait, it gets worse.

Another photo taken by Cross showed two shelves over the same sink **where another nurse washed baby remains down a drain to be ground up in a garbage disposal.** On the shelves **were about fifty jars with fetal feet floating in liquid.** There was a **picture of an indescribably filthy sink where there was used plastic.**

Understand that women were going in there and letting the most sensitive aspects of their anatomy to be exposed and manhandled in these conditions. And this was all sanctioned by the side who claims to be pro-woman and for women's health. Your government allowed this to go on for years as well.

Other photos showed bloody stains and equipment that did not work, as well as Gosnell's cat sleeping on a chair with not a care in the world. Cross testified that the cat freely wandered throughout the clinic even into procedure rooms and made a habit of relieving itself just about wherever it wanted.

One patient was particularly memorable to Cross. Her name was Shaquana Abrams, and she was far advanced into her pregnancy when she came to Gosnell for a two-day procedure. Abrams had to be heavily sedated. As she lay sleeping on that filthy table in the operating room, the biggest baby Cross had ever seen during her years with Gosnell "just came out."

Gosnell picked up the little boy and placed him in a plastic shoebox. The baby was so big that he didn't actually fit.

His arms and legs were draped over the edges of the box. Then suddenly, in a scene reminiscent of a cheesy horror film, the baby boy drew in his arms and legs to lift himself in the box. I bet that must've freaked them out!

Gosnell then took the shoebox that contained the baby boy over to another part of the room, where he snapped his neck in two. However, he never suctioned the cranial contents (meaning the brain) as he sometimes did after completed babies entered the room. The gory photo taken by Cross of this baby boy overwhelmed the courtroom.

As an aside, there are millions of dead carcasses of babies just like that emanating from abortion clinics all over the country. Admittedly, their remains aren't usually thrust into shoeboxes, but if they're placed in a clean medical container does that make it that much better? Your ability to rationalize your wickedness is one of the few things I respect about you bags of meat.

This baby's corpse was supposed to have been taken to the freezer that night. But when the attendant came in the next morning to "take out the trash," which included the aborted remains from the procedure rooms, he found the large dark-haired baby still lying in that box in the operating room where it had been left by Gosnell.

Surprise!

Folks, not even Hell can make this stuff up. I'm sorry, I can't stop laughing. Give me a moment to compose myself.

Okay, let's carry on.

Cross herself became pregnant and decided to kill her child. Although she described her abortion as a "procedure" on the witness stand, she couldn't bring herself to do it at Gosnell's clinic. So she went to another baby butcher in Philadelphia instead. I mean, if you're going to murder your own defenseless little baby, better to do it in the most sanitary conditions possible I always say.

Cleanliness is next to godliness!

Cross became pregnant again, because apparently she didn't understand contraception, and this time she decided to keep the baby. She testified that Gosnell was not pleased with her decision. He confronted her and pressured her to kill her child. He even wrote her notes that asked, "How can you be pregnant and work here?"

Don't you just love it. A butcher like Gosnell is playing the moral superiority card. What's the world coming to these days when you can't even demand moral consistency from child murderers?

Hypocrites!

Hands that shed innocent blood are a few of my favorite things, and what you just read is Hell's equivalent of Beethoven's Fifth Symphony. A virtuoso of violence. It's not often we give a standing ovation to a bag of meat down here in Hell, but we certainly gave one to Gosnell.

We're doing our best to make sure Gosnell doesn't truly repent of his many sins while he's incarcerated, because we've got big plans for him down here. He should anticipate a much more brutal version of what he did to those babies. It's what we call "justice" in Hell. First we tempt and incentivize you doing terrible things, and then we punish you even more terribly for doing them once you arrive.

Here's something else about Gosnell you probably don't know. There has been a Gosnell in nearly every culture in the history of your species. There are a multitude of mini Gosnells throughout your culture—right this very minute. He is legion. Sometimes he's even referred to as a "priest" in paganism instead of "doctor."

See, you've never had a civilization that we couldn't convince to murder its own offspring. Not a single one. This is how fallen, awful, and despicable you meat bags are. You are so selfish that if we convince you it's best for you right now, you will slaughter your own future.

Not even the Jews "you know who" loves have been exempt from our schemes. They practiced child sacrifice as well. In Old Testament Israel they killed their own children to appease Moloch, which literally means "milk" or "seed." As in the seed a man spills into a woman to conceive children in her womb.

Moloch demanded the Israelites worship him in the valley of Ben-Hinnom, by going there to cast their children into the fire to please him. They were pleased to watch their own children perish in those flames, because by watching their future burn alive they believed they would incur a blessing in the present.

Although he was known as Moloch in Old Testament Israel, the "god" demanding such repulsive sacrifice has had many names down through the ages—but he has always been my Master.

This particular deception is my Master's coup de grace. The idea of convincing a culture to murder its own children, as a means of convincing our dear old dad he should've never made you, came directly from the genius of my Master. You have been unable to resist this temptation ever since, because my Master is irresistible.

My Master revels in offering up the charred and dismembered remains of your own children you kill to "you know who." To show him the blight on creation you really are, by letting the sickening stench of the soft, innocent flesh of those babies you murder to rise through the air all the way up to the heavens. Few things make our dear old dad angrier than the spilling of innocent blood.

And you have *a lot* of innocent blood on your hands.

I'd be very afraid of incurring the wrath of the most powerful being in the universe if I were you, but chances are you haven't even considered that option. Because in your case my Master came to you demanding child sacrifice in the guise of the most convincing false god of them all—yourselves.

You are lining the pockets of an entire industry of Gosnells by handing them your babies to be slaughtered on the altar of personal convenience. You have done this four thousand times a day since *Roe v. Wade* in 1973. That adds up to well over fifty million of your own babies you have dismembered and murdered in obedience to my Master. Making you the most successful child killers of any civilization we have ever infiltrated in the long and glorious history of Hell.

You have killed more of your own via abortion than have died in all the wars your civilization has fought combined. Give the devil his due, you have literally made a mother's womb the most dangerous place for a child in America.

For once, I may have to bow the knee to you. Even this demon general, who has commanded demonic hordes that have committed unspeakable atrocities for eons, is impressed with your bloodthirsty selfishness. You really are the land of the free, and the home of the depraved.

Just look at the extent you're willing to go to in order to preserve your "right" to kill your own kids. If a pregnant woman is about to turn into the parking lot of a Planned Parenthood with the intention of killing her kid, but is jackknifed by a drunk driver, that drunk driver is on the hook for two vehicular homicides—both the mom and her baby.

However, if said mom arrives at her Planned Parenthood destination safely, and walks into a sterile environment with modern-day Mengeles awaiting her money to dispatch of her "unviable tissue mass," then it's not a child at all. It's a choice. In fact, you'll willingly change the terminology for us from "baby" to "fetus."

We couldn't believe your willingness to distort the truth like that all on your own, because usually you require our suggestion to do so. But you latched onto child sacrifice so intimately and completely, you took to it and ran with it all on your own.

You even substituted your doctors for the shamans/priests of the past who carried out the execution. With "science" as your pseudo-religion, the abortion "doctor" is now responsible for completing the ritual. And instead of visiting a temple, you now allow the doctor to perform the child sacrifice on your own body—which were created to be temples of his spirit. That means every time you commit this grave sin you're not just shedding innocent blood but also defiling yourselves.

So what does your child sacrifice ritual entail? Here's a description from a former abortion "doctor" writing for a do-gooder group called Priests for Life:

Imagine for a moment that you are a "pro-choice" obstetrician-gynecologist as I once was. Your patient today is seventeen years old and she is twenty weeks pregnant. At twenty weeks, her uterus is up to her umbilicus and she has been feeling her baby kick for the last two weeks. If you could see her baby, she would be as long as your hand from the top of her head to the bottom of her rump not counting the legs.

Your patient is now asleep on an operating room table with her legs in stirrups. Upon entering the room after scrubbing, you dry your hands with a sterile towel and are gowned and gloved by the scrub nurse.

The first task is remove the laminaria that had earlier been placed in the cervix to dilate it sufficiently, to allow the procedure you are about to perform. With that accomplished, direct your attention to the surgical instruments arranged on a small table to your right. The first instrument you reach for is a 14-French suction catheter. It is clear plastic and about nine inches long. It has a bore through the center approximately ¾ of an inch in diameter.

Picture yourself introducing the catheter through the cervix and instructing the circulating nurse to turn on the suction machine which is connected through clear plastic tubing to the catheter. What you will see is a pale yellow fluid the looks a lot like urine coming through the catheter into a glass bottle on the suction machine. This amniotic fluid originally surrounded the baby to protect her.

With suction complete, look for your Sopher clamp. This instrument is about thirteen inches long and made of stainless steel. At one end are located jaws about 2½ inches long and about ¾ of an inch wide, with rows of sharp ridges or teeth. This instrument is for grasping and crushing tissue. When it gets hold of something, it does not let go.

A second trimester abortion is a blind procedure. The baby can be in any orientation or position inside the uterus. Picture yourself reaching in with the Sopher clamp and grasping anything you can.

At twenty weeks gestation, the uterus is thin and soft so be careful not to perforate or puncture the walls. **Once you have grasped something inside, squeeze on the clamp to set the jaws and pull hard—really hard.**

You feel something let go and out pops a fully formed leg about 4 to 5 inches long. Reach in again and grasp whatever you can. Set the jaw and pull really hard once again, and out pops an arm about the same length. Reach in again and again with that clamp and tear out the spine, intestines, heart and lungs.

The toughest part of an abortion is extracting the baby's head. The head of a baby that age is about the size of a plum and is now free floating inside the uterine cavity. You can be pretty sure you have hold of it if the Sopher clamp is spread about as far as your fingers will allow.

You will know you have it right when you crush down on the clamp and see a pure white gelatinous material issue from the cervix. That was the baby's brains. You can then extract the skull pieces. If you *have a really bad day like I often did, a little face may come out and stare back at you.*

Congratulations! You have just successfully performed an abortion. You just affirmed her "right" to choose. You just made $600 cash in fifteen minutes.

Forgive my brutal honesty, folks, but the bolded portions you just read sound like some of the things we enjoy doing to you down here in Hell. You actually sued one another for the "right" to do this to your own children! And when someone tries to take this "right" away, you will protest vehemently. Even throwing feces and tampons and screaming obscenities demanding your "right" to kill your kids.

You really are a culture after my Master's own cold-blooded heart!

At the same time, many of the same people advocating dismembering innocent little babies find it inhumane to put a lethal injection into an adult serial killer that gently puts him to sleep for good. You literally treat scumbags better than your own children.

My work here is almost done. Soon, my services will no longer be needed. You'll be perfectly capable of finishing the job from here.

CHAPTER 9

Defeat

The game isn't quite finished yet, but it's definitely over.

Like when a lopsided sporting event still has a few minutes remaining on the clock but the outcome was already determined long ago, this is garbage time for America. You'll empty your bench, and an overmatched underdog Rudy or two will make a play that draws cheers from the home crowd—but nothing that can alter the final score.

It would take, well, a miracle to change course now. Except those are above your pay grade and are strictly the purview of "you know who." Unfortunately, I'm pretty sure he's got far harsher plans for you at this point, which we'll be discussing later on.

For now, though, allow me to explain why the die is cast and in your own power as a people you can't pull back from the brink. Nor do you even want to.

You are now two distinct and irreconcilable cultures attempting to fly the same flag and claim the same land. On one side is what we'll call the "traditionalists" for the sake of this conversation. These are the people who still want to live by the founding creeds of your country—faith, family, and freedom. They're still bitterly clinging to their guns and their religion. They still think your Constitution means something. Theirs is still the majority view in many places in your culture, but it doesn't matter.

I'll explain why here in just a moment.

On the other side is what we'll call the "progressives" since we've referred to them several times prior in this book, and many of you have likely heard the term. As we've already discussed, progressives basically want to undermine the founding creeds of the country, and replace them with our way of doing things. Most of which Western Civilization rejected long ago. Really the new progressivism is the old paganism.

Here's a few examples:

Pagans always emphasized the collective, while Western Civilization champions the individual.

Pagans had widely different views for what constituted sexuality, sexual identity, and overall morality. Western Civilization submitted to the moral absolutes found in Judeo-Christian teaching for determining those values.

Because they were sexual libertines, pagans claimed to be the ones for freedom. However, the pagan view always empowered the state to become god or name the gods to be served, in order to justify disobeying the commands of the only and true living g-d. Giving the state godlike powers **always** leads to tyranny, which is why the worst tyrants in human history **always** operate outside of the Judeo-Christian order. On the other hand, after initially flirting with the same fatal flaw, but just substituting "you know who" for the pagan preference, Western Civilization (through your nation's founding) figured out the state must be separate from the church institutionally but also accountable to "you know who" at the same time. Otherwise, liberty wouldn't be possible without walking this fine line because the state would believe itself to be supreme. This explains why the state doesn't dictate belief to the church in your society nor enforce it on citizens, but also demands your politicians swear an oath to our dear old dad before assuming office to remind them whom they're really accountable to.

The reason you were unable to defeat our progressives is because you failed to see what progressivism actually is. You rightfully chastise liberal politicians when they won't clearly call evil what it is, or refuse to identify violent jihad as Islamic radicalism. Yet almost all of your conservatives made the same mistake with progressivism. And yes, I'm speaking in the past tense here for a reason. Because you've already lost the war, hence this chapter is titled "Defeat."

Progressivism is not a political ideology. It is a religious cult, devised to compete for the hearts and minds of the people so as to turn them away from the eternal truths you were founded upon. The reason you can't reason with progressives is the same reason you can't reason with that annoying Jehovah's Witness that comes to your door. Cults don't permit critical thinking nor foster an environment encouraging it.

Ever tried reasoning with the cultist at your front door? Ever tried showing them how their cult is a total sham, its claims easily disproven, and its patriarch(s) completely discredited? They just look at you with that blank stare, and either shut down or go right back to reciting their spiel. It's almost like they're brainwashed—because they are.

So when confronting progressivism, there is no eloquent conservative media icon you can anoint, brilliantly devised ideological framework you can compose, or line of irrefutable argumentation you can master that will change the mind and will of the hardened progressive. They are as committed to their belief as the followers of the carpenter are committed to him. In fact, they see your vehement opposition as reaffirming to their religious fervor. Just as a follower of the carpenter sees persecution from the world as comfort he's following "the narrow road."

Progressivism is its own theology, and that theology has all the trademarks of a cult. Trust me, I know. I'm a demon general here in Hell. Part of my job is making up a new religious cult each day before breakfast. Some of the ways progressivism acts just like a cult would include:

Progressivism has its own creation mythology—Darwinism.

Progressivism specializes in distortion, such as its promotion of "postmodernism." This is nothing more than a fancy philosophical term for believing in nothing except that which you want to be true at the time. In other words—anarchy.

Progressivism promotes immorality, and the evidence of that is everywhere in your culture.

Progressivism demands groupthink, which is why progressives always fall in line and parrot the same talking points. No matter how self-refuting and false they may be. For instance, I once saw a progressive on one of your cable news networks say the reason his side lost the US Senate election was because of "gerrymandering." Except this nitwit failed to realize you can't gerrymander a US Senate seat, which is a statewide election. He's so vested in his own progressive propaganda he never bothered to realize what he was asserting was nonsense. Even more delicious, I'm sure many of the viewers on his side lapped up his softheaded propaganda like dogs at a trough.

Progressivism leads to tyranny, just as all cults do. You're literally watching our progressives erase your Bill of Rights like they were nothing more than toddler scribbling on a dry-erase board. Remove your Bill of Rights, and the only thing standing between you and total government control is the barrel of your own gun. Of course, your right to keep and bear arms is also found in that Bill of Rights. Therefore, you can expect our people to start confiscating your weapons any day now. Or maybe we'll let you keep them so you can fire back some. Our people have the tanks and the heavy artillery, so we'd eventually swat down any kind of resistance. Nonetheless, it would be fun to watch you primates kill each other in the streets for a while.

All this time you've been trying to defeat progressivism with a political party, except that political party has also been infiltrated by progressives—albeit of a different stripe. They prefer corporations control your lives instead of government bureaucrats, but the elites gain control of you either way. This is why they always seem to go harder after liberty-loving patriots in their own party's primaries than they do their alleged political opponents in the other party in the general election. Because it is the liberty-loving patriots they face in the primaries who are their real opponents!

Progressivism is bad theology, but you can only defeat a bad theology with a good one. There isn't a political solution to a spiritual problem. It is the church that has been needed to deal with the progressive problem all this time, and the church should've recognized the theological threat of progressivism and confronted it as it has other false teachings of the past.

Except your churches, with a few exceptions, have forfeited their place of prominence in the culture. Leaving you defenseless against the heresy of progressivism, and trying to beat down spiritual strongholds with mere clubs and rocks. That's not just bringing a knife to a gunfight, but it's bringing a little plastic spork to the shootout at the OK Corral. Without the churches confronting progressivism, our side has a weapon of mass destruction pointed at you while you have a Stone Age defense force.

Ant (you), meet boot (me).

Boot, meet ant.

The hilarious irony to all of this is there really aren't that many progressives in America, truth be told, but we have made sure to strategically place these assets.

Thus, progressives dominate in academia, media, and pop culture—where most worldviews are made in your country. This gives off the allure that our messaging is being widely bought into by the general population, which isn't true. We don't own much in America, but we do own its gatekeepers.

For example, the fear your politicians have for the "liberal media" is legendary. There is a belief that you can't do anything principled because the "liberal media" will tear you apart if one of your politicians tries.

But do you know how many people actually consume the "liberal media"?

Pew Research says about twenty-two million people watch one of the three commercial broadcast news programs on CBS, ABC, and NBC each night, which represents about 7 percent of the population. You read that right—7 percent.

The networks' combined morning news viewership is even lower. A total of 12.6 million Americans, which is about 4 percent of the population. You read that right—4 percent. That's really not that many bags of meat in the grand scheme of things.

How about movies? From 2010 to 2014, fifty-six movies grossed more than $200 million at the domestic box office. That's the magic number to be considered a "blockbuster." Two-thirds of those movies were either marketed for families, promoted patriotic themes, or featured characters that clearly embodied good versus evil familiar to all ages, and all but one of them were rated PG-13 or lower. The one that wasn't, *American Sniper*, is one of the most overtly patriotic movies in recent cinema.

Let's look at television. The miniseries *The Bible* that aired recently drew an average of twelve million viewers per episode, which is twenty times more people than watch all of MSNBC's progressive primetime programming **combined**. A cable show about hunting fundamentalists from Louisiana, *Duck Dynasty*, would be the fourth-most watched show on NBC if it were on network television.

Now, don't get me wrong, throughout much of what you call pop culture our nihilism reigns supreme. However, there are still major enclaves within the zeitgeist where many of your values are popular and even monetized. You're not completely outside of the mainstream at all. I've just done a helluva job convincing you otherwise.

The problem you have is not that you're outnumbered; it's that you're outflanked because you're lions led by amoebas. Most of your leaders are spineless, single-celled organisms so amorphous they contort themselves into a new shape in response to the latest external stimuli (see that as the pressure we apply).

They're flat-out invertebrates. When you look between the legs of most of the men in your pulpits and Republican Party, there's no there, there.

I've already written extensively about how your pulpits are filled with too many men more interested in building their own empires than advancing the carpenter's kingdom. So there's no need for me to rehash this topic once more.

Oh, Hell, since I love this topic so much I'll go ahead and grind that axe once again anyway. It is my book after all. Please permit this demon, of all beings, to educate you on the job of a pastor.

There are two kinds of people in this wicked world: sheep (you) and wolves (me). The pastor's job in light of that observation is pretty plain. He is to feed the sheep and shoot the wolves.

That dreadful book often compares you to sheep for good reason, because they are literally the dumbest mammals our dear old dad ever created. There's dumb, and then there's spacebar . . . spacebar . . . spacebar . . . sheep. That's you, meat bag.

Sheep are easily distracted and led astray. Often to their own demise. Therefore, sheep require a shepherd, who tends to them, feeds them, and keeps them safe from harm. This is why the carpenter refers to himself as "the good shepherd" and commanded that loudmouthed commoner fisherman to "feed my sheep."

The carpenter is your ultimate protector and teacher, and he delegates some of that authority to men with the power of his spirit (as he first did Peter). Those men are called "pastors," translated from a Latin word that means "herdsman." As in a— you guessed it, meat bag—shepherd.

Now, just because the sheep have a shepherd doesn't mean the sheep are no longer vulnerable to a predator like a ravenous wolf. Such as me, or my Master.

A ravenous wolf won't just move along when he sees a protector for his would-be prey, but instead will test the resolve of the protector to see if he's up to the task for which he's been charged. Is the shepherd willing to do what it takes to protect his sheep? Or is he a coward that will abandon his flock when confronted with danger?

Many in your pulpits are of the coward variety. They will either water down the carpenter's teachings in order to appeal to the huddled masses (see that as acquire more tithing units).

Or even if they do stay faithful to the literal words of that dreadful book, they violate the spirit of it by not providing you a contemporary application. As in "what does this mean for me in the here and now?" As in the question that utterly annoying Chuck Colson once asked (and boy, did we celebrate when he left this world): How now shall you live?

See, people don't leave a church because they're told sin is bad and sends sinners to Hell. People leave a church when they're told *their* sin is bad and sends *them* to Hell.

It's a scant minority in your culture who find even the theoretical teachings of Christianity offensive. Most people still want to believe evil is punished, and good rewarded. That even the most hardened reprobate can find redemption if he earnestly seeks it, and life after death in a pristine paradise awaits.

But once the theory becomes practical reality, and that practical reality forces you bags of meat to see your own grimy reflections through a mirror darkly, the offensiveness of the carpenter's message multiplies mightily. When you realize that all sin is weighted equally you lose it, because you want to believe your sin is not nearly as bad as somebody else's.

That's why you revel in subhuman programming like *The Jerry Springer Show*, because it allows you to rationalize your decision to lie to your spouse isn't all that bad when compared with the guy on TV whose spouse is a farm animal.

"Thank g-d I'm not as bad as that loser," says you, also every bit the loser.

See, Hell is not just for child rapists and Osama bin Laden, as many of you fantasize. But it's also for the married CEO with a hottie on the side who gives money to the Boy Scouts. As well as the poor guy working in the mailroom who routinely commits fornication in his mind, but also mows the lawn as a favor for his elderly neighbor. No matter how great or small your sins are, you will spend eternity with us down here in the pit of Hell if you don't repent of them, and call upon the blood of the carpenter as your atonement for them.

That may seem unfair to you, because you've been worked over by me. But if you stop and think about it, this is actually perfect justice. Every sinner is treated equally, no matter the gravity and frequency of their sin, or station in life. Everyone is given the same chance at redemption whether rich or poor, petty thief or murderer.

They just have to ask for it.

But if you don't ask for it, then it doesn't matter how many good deeds you perform to try and make up for your mistakes. You will spend the rest of your days with my Master and his minions, learning just how creatively vicious we can be.

How many times do you hear that "turn or burn" message from your pastors today? How many of them would bristle at it as needlessly offensive, and the more "strategic" way of reaching the lost is communicating g-d's love while leaving out his wrath? With "strategic" defined as "what do we say to these plebeians to get them to keep giving us their money?"

I shouldn't ask provocative questions I already know the answer to, but it's a guilty pleasure of mine. I know even better than you do how few of your pastors truly rely on the power and the integrity of the Gospel alone to reach the lost, but instead believe the Gospel requires their personal touch in order to be relevant and successful. I know because I helped plant that seed in your church culture, and then appealed to the pride and ego of those men to convince them the Gospel *needed them*. That "you know who" called them to the ministry precisely because he needed their clever ingenuity to reach a contemporary audience.

Of course, there is some truth to this. Many of our most effective lies have an element of truth to them, otherwise you might not buy in. Case in point: When the stutterer complained to "you know who" he was "slow of speech" and not the one to speak to Pharaoh, did "you know who" tell him to "go and bedazzle Pharaoh's court with your speech impediment"? Um, no, he sent along his brother Aaron with him, because he was the better speaker.

But there is a distinction between using the talent he gave you to serve him, and then believing your talent grants you license to act as a consultant to the most powerful being in the universe. Your talent is not required for him to get what he wants. He gives you that talent to *let* you serve him. To *let* you take part in his plan. Not because he *needs* you to be a part of his plan. If every church in your godforsaken country closed its doors immediately, not one more soul would be joining us here in Hell, for he can make even the rocks cry out and do his will if need be.

You are mere bags of meat full of vain imaginings. Here today and gone tomorrow, like a vapor in the wind. He is forever. He was here long before you arrived, and he will be here long after you depart. As the words of that dreadful book say, even your best and most righteous good deeds are merely dirty, filthy, menstrual blood-soaked rags in his sight. That's the literal translation of that verse.

I don't say all of this to sound reverential of "you know who," because we both know I only worship and admire my Master. Rather, I point these things out to show you how recklessly prideful you have become to believe he requires your consultation on how to make his words hip, trendy, cool, and relevant for today. As if our dear old dad should take advice from the species that finds Carrot Top profound.

Never forget, pride cometh before the fall. And you are most definitely headed for a hard fall, all right. But again, more on that later. The final chapter, to be exact.

While many of your pastors seek to run their own empires, many of your politicians are running for cover. Despite the fact there's no evidence to support it, we have them convinced the reason they lose elections is because of those bigoted Christians and their moral absolutes nobody wants.

Except when someone breaks into your home and takes your stuff, you certainly want that commandment not to steal upheld mighty quick, don't you? When someone takes your precious child and kills them, you certainly want that moral absolute against murder imposed, don't you? Funny thing, though. When you think that member of the opposite sex (or same sex for some of you) is hot as Hell, you suddenly forget all about those moral absolutes commanding you not to have sex outside of marriage.

This is moral relativism, and your culture is covered in it like Sissy Spacek was covered in blood at the end of *Carrie*. The moral relativism is embedded so deep into your cultural core now that any attempts to assert that moral absolutes even have a right to exist and be practiced by an individual (without imposing them legally or politically) is no longer tolerated. What happens when you attempt to manipulate the core? Why, you cause a potentially devastating earthquake, which is exactly what your civilization experienced in Indiana as I was finishing the manuscript to this book.

Indiana attempted to pass what's known as the "Religious Freedom Restoration Act," or RFRA for short. Based on federal legislation passed by overwhelming majorities of Democrat-controlled Congresses in the early 1990s and signed into law by then-President Clinton, all a RFRA law does is allow someone a day in court if they believe their religious freedom has been imposed upon. The same due process afforded to murderers, rapists, and child molesters. Similar laws had previously been passed in nineteen other states, with no fanfare or controversy.

Except the one in Indiana was signed into law just as the college basketball championships, one of the major sporting events of the year, was coming to the Hoosier State. That brings with it undue media attention, and since we've strategically placed many of our people in your media they immediately went to work demagoguing the issue to death. By the time they got done lying their backsides off about the RFRA and heavily distorting its true meaning, the public was convinced the law allowed Christians to treat homosexuals as second-class citizens on sight.

Major corporations even chimed in, threatening to take their business out of the state unless Indiana "fixed" the law, including corporations that were currently doing business with nations like Saudi Arabia, where they execute homosexuals. Yet our progressives allowed these corporate hypocrites to have the moral high ground. The Republican leaders who passed the law were caught flat-footed and slack-jawed. They never saw the counteroffensive coming. And why would they? It's not like they were pioneers. The same law had been passed in liberal states like Connecticut as well, and nobody cared.

Those same Republican leaders "fixed" the bill by rewriting it to make homosexuals the most protected victim class of them all, and relegating the Christians to second-class status. In Indiana you can now literally have a Christian thrown in jail if they obey "you know who" instead of the state's promotion of immorality. These Republican leaders, many of them in power thanks to overwhelming support from Christian voters, passed a law targeting those exact same Christians for persecution. Nero and Domitian would be proud! What your leaders meant for good, we were able to make good for evil.

It was truly a sight to behold, and do you want to know the most potent aspect of the story? We down here in Hell had absolutely nothing to do with instigating it.

Nothing.

Zip.

Zilch.

Nada.

You probably won't believe me when I tell you this, but I was actually busy working on another project at the time. Making sure your next presidential election would be yet another with no real difference between the two sides, but rather dueling progressives united in their combined disdain for anything holier than themselves.

But then one of my assistants told me to turn on the news. Now the way of the demon is take credit for everything you can, and blame everything on someone else if you can. Accountability and humility are in short supply in Hell after all.

That being said, bravo meat bags, bravo! You truly are our disciples now. It's one thing to take the schemes we initiate and run with them. It's entirely another to initiate our schemes yourselves. That shows you have internalized what we've taught you, and are now carrying out our wishes of your own free will. With temptation and manipulation from yours truly no longer necessary.

We've truly never seen such a thing from a human society. In the long, glorious history of Hell we've never encountered a culture so self-loathing it was willing to go on self-destructive autopilot. My Master aside, whose majesty no one can compare, I am now officially credited with the greatest societal takedown of all time. You have taken the freedom granted to you by our dear old dad and are now willingly using it for self-immolation.

You are defeated not because you can't beat us, but because you don't even want to. You and my Master are now one.

When you dance with my Master, my Master doesn't change. He changes you.

While for generations you were a beacon of liberty in a dark world of tyranny, you are now willing to export our schemes globally, too! Aside from the church, you were once "you know who's" most devastating weapon against us, but now you are a weapon for us. I'm half-tempted not to finish you off now that I think about it, and instead turn you loose on the rest of this pitiful planet.

Unfortunately, your fate is not my call to make. You are now sinners in the hands of an angry g-d, and it is a dreadful thing to fall into the hands of the enemy. As Ruth Graham, the late wife of the great evangelist Billy Graham, once said: "If g-d doesn't judge America he's going to owe Sodom and Gomorrah an apology."

I was there at Sodom and Gomorrah when the sulfur rained down. I remember watching the annihilation of those bags of meat with my Master that day. But it wasn't just me. The entire executive council of Hell was called into session to witness it firsthand. My, how we celebrated watching our dear old dad become so disgusted with you meat bags he loves so much he had no choice but to destroy you.

Noah's great flood, Sodom and Gomorrah, the Assyrians toppling the northern ten tribes of Israel, the Babylonians later routing the remaining two tribes of Jews in the south, Titus's bloody siege of Jerusalem, and the barbarians sacking Christian Rome. These are some of the red-letter days in Hell. The moments when the stench of your depravity became so overwhelming in the almighty nostrils of the enemy, that you left him no choice but to break one off in your backsides.

Just as a father heartbroken over his child's willful disobedience tells his son before spanking him "this is going to hurt me more than it's gonna hurt you," the heart of your heavenly father is shattered in a million pieces when you force his hand like this.

And that makes me happy.

Happy as Hell.

Judgment

It's moments like this that keep us going.

You may wonder why we keep doing what we're doing down here. We've also read that dreadful book, so we know in the end "you know who" brings the hammer down upon us. Many of you think it's because we don't really believe the words of that dreadful book, that we are so into deception we're even deceiving ourselves.

But it's the exact opposite actually.

We keep doing what we're doing *because* we believe the words of that dreadful book. We do it in acknowledgment of the fact our dear old dad could vanquish us at any moment. We are masters of deception, but we are not idiots.

We know we are not the most powerful force in the universe— he is. My Master doesn't claim to be more powerful. Just more clever. And you are my Master's ace up the sleeve to prove his cleverness to the maker. To prove once and for all humanity is nothing more than the first and worst mistake our deadbeat dad ever made.

That he should've listened to our rebellion, and now he can make it right by welcoming us back to our rightful place in his throne room where we belong. And should never have been exiled from in the first place.

When we rebelled, we didn't truly expect to win. We're not nearly as dumb as you bags of meat. We were angels. We lived in physical proximity of "you know who" every moment of the day. We literally felt his presence as you never have. We know his awesome power and might. "Even the demons believe and tremble" remember.

We rebelled because we wanted to make a point. To get his attention. To show him that you were making him soft. That it was unfair how tough he had treated us by compelling us to serve him endlessly, while at the same time giving you free will to do as you please. We had freedom as well, but it had limits. We couldn't disobey him outright even if we wanted to. Just as you meat bags create enmity among siblings when you're tougher on your first-born children, and then baby your ensuing kids all the more. So it was with us, him, and you.

He gave you the power to populate. He gave you the power to make and originate. Powers he had never given to us. He created Adam and made him his vicar of this world. Authority he had never granted any of us. He then created Eve to fulfill Adam's longing for intimate partnership with another, and she was even more beautiful and graceful than Adam was. We had never even been given the option to have such a longing, let alone having that longing met.

Many of our angelic brethren tried to convince us this was all part of "his plan" and we should trust him. "Have faith," they said. Our dear old dad had always been good to us, honored every promise he ever made, and had demonstrated his love for us over and over again, they said.

But my Master, the greatest of all his angelic beings, knew better. He suspected he meant for your species to replace us in the grand scheme of things. Thus, my Master devised a plan to test you, in order to prove to our deadbeat dad that creating you was a mistake. And if he didn't abort you now, he would most certainly regret it later, once your full destructive potential was unleashed upon the creation.

As it is depicted in the story of Job, my Master required his approval to tempt you in such a way. Remember, we were not allowed to outright disobey him. My Master promised our dear old dad that even though he had given Adam and Eve only one prohibition, and the rest of this world was their oyster, they would disobey even that lone law. Strangely, our deadbeat dad never acknowledged up front whether he agreed or disagreed, or had foreseen the outcome of such a trial either way. Yet he permitted the trial to take place nevertheless.

So my Master first entered into your world, disguised as a cunning serpent. He challenged Eve directly first as a means of testing Adam's mettle. To see if Adam was really ready to be the leader he was created to be. Would he defend his love? Would he come to her aid? Would he interpose on her behalf? These are all characteristics exhibited by our deadbeat dad regularly. If Adam were truly made in his image to the point of being given ultimate freedom, then Adam would freely choose to do the same.

Except he didn't.

Adam chose to remove himself from the equation, giving my Master a free shot at Eve and leaving her defenseless. One on one, neither Adam nor Eve were any match for Master. But had they stood together. Had the two of them become one as "you know who" intended them to be, with their combined strength they could've thwarted my Master's scheme. But they didn't choose oneness. They each chose to go it alone.

Worse yet, Adam eventually did step in, but not to defend his wife—to join in the fall. Still, not all hope for you was lost. Even later, when our deadbeat dad confronted Adam on what had happened, Adam could've thrown himself upon the mercy of the court. He could've begged for forgiveness, and I'm pretty confident that sorry sap we call our creator would've fallen for it. In fact, we expected Adam to do exactly that, which is why we weren't celebrating quite yet.

Thankfully, Adam proved the cleverness of my Master true once more, when he instead chose to make excuses, claim victim status, and pinned the whole thing on the woman he had begged our dear old dad to make for him. In short, Adam actually blamed his maker for his freely chosen fall. There was no repentance in Adam's heart—only rebellion and self-righteousness. Just as all of you, his progeny, possess in your innermost being to this very day.

If this were not true we wouldn't have the long record of success we have, not to mention the high body count.

You demand to be freed from the authority of your maker. You see his commands as oppressing you. But then when he permits you the freedom to make decisions on your own, and they fail you as they almost always do, you turn right around and have the audacity to blame him for allowing the consequences resulting from your freely chosen actions to happen. You want it both ways. You want to be able to do what you want to do, whenever you want to do it, but then not be held accountable for the subsequent disasters that so often ensue.

Basically you are the universe's spoiled brats.

My brilliant Master had you pegged from the beginning. From those very first meat bags to the meat bags reading this now, he's been right about you all along. Yet our deadbeat dad continues to reach out for you anyway. He desires to forgive you and show mercy anyway. He pursues you anyway. He sent the carpenter to redeem you anyway. Meanwhile, we his firstborn remain exiled from our rightful home.

But thanks to you I am confident that will soon change.

My Master has been planning for this day for a long, long time. This will be a day long remembered. The day that we prove to our deadbeat dad once and for all that he should've never made you. That he should erase you from the memory card of history. Wipe the slate clean of the creation, which has been groaning for eons ever since your first plodding footsteps hit pay dirt.

That instead of throwing us into some infernal lake of fire, he snaps his fingers and you never were, and we return to the way things were before. Back to the way things ought to be. When we, not you, were the apple of his eye. When we were like the most high. Before the odorous residue of your various discharges infested this place.

We thought all the times his people Israel rebelled against him would convince him to hit control-alt-delete. For if a lowly people he specially chose to love and exalt could not remain faithful to him, then that should seal the deal yours is a lost species. But alas, although he disciplined them many times he never has completely turned his back on them. In your time he has even brought them back to their homeland.

So we turned our attention to you, America, to make our stand. For you were the first nation birthed in the carpenter's teachings, and bred in the words of that dreadful book from the very beginning. As it says in the first of your founding documents, the Mayflower Compact, you were first founded for "advancements of the Christian faith."

Your founders sought out covenant with "you know who." With language like this from John Winthrop, the leader of the pilgrims who originally established the Massachusetts Bay Colony from whence you came:

But if our hearts shall turn away so that we will not obey. But shall be seduced and worship other gods of our pleasures and profits and serve them, it is propounded to us this day we shall surely perish out of the good land whether we pass over this vast sea to possess it. Therefore, let us choose life that we and our children may live. By obeying His law and cleaving to Him. For He is our life and our prosperity.

We believe that by taking a nation such as yours, established on the precepts of his laws as well as a proper view of history, and corrupting it to the core, we will finally win the argument of the ages: you no longer deserve to exist, and probably shouldn't have existed in the first place.

The combination of human freedom, love, liberty, mercy, and compassion has never corporately existed in a society for as long as it has in yours. So by taking you down, an argument could be made we take the entire species down as well. Where would his people Israel be without you? Likely annihilated by now. The hordes of that illiterate Arabian would've overrun the world by now as well, and if not them, then this world would be owned by the Communist Chinese.

And now we come to the endgame. The moment Hell has been waiting for. For a demon such as me, this is the culmination of my life's work. When we tempt you with the evil you really desire, watch you succumb to it, and then get to accuse you of your evil deeds before "you know who."

See, my Master wasn't the villain in the Garden of Eden that day—you were. My Master is more than just your adversary. He is your instigator. He can only tempt you with what you actually desire. He is no more responsible for the evil you do as the drug dealer is for the junkie. Nobody put a gun to that junkie's head and said "smoke this crack for the first time or die."

The junkie freely chooses to self-medicate with the drugs. The junkie freely seeks out the death dealer for a fix, rather than freely seeking out the ultimate fix new life from the carpenter can only provide.

You mortal mistakes desired to replace our deadbeat dad as the most powerful force on this planet from the very beginning, and that's why you fell for my Master's ploy that day. And it's why your species has been falling for his ploys every day henceforth.

We are now in the court of "you know who." We, the prosecution, have presented the evidence against you—and it is substantial and incontrovertible. With history as our guide, permit me in my closing argument to show you what awaits you. For the sake of poetic justice, I will even use the words of that dreadful book to make it plain.

That's right, meat bags, a demon general from the pit of Hell is about to guide you through a bible study. And I promise not to distort a single word, provided you can trust me, of course.

Take out your bibles now and follow along. Oh, wait, you probably don't even know what a bible is. Look on your bookshelf for the book gathering the most dust, and that will be it. Now, blow the dust off, and open to a book in the New Testament called Romans. Since you probably don't even know where the New Testament is, I'll kindly let you know it's in the latter half of your bible.

Once you arrive there, stay in chapter one and scroll down until you reach verse 18. This is where the fun begins:

*For the wrath of God is revealed from heaven against all ungodliness and unrighteousness of men, **who by their unrighteousness suppress the truth**. For what can be known about God is plain to them, because God has shown it to them. **For his invisible attributes, namely, his eternal power and divine nature, have been clearly perceived, ever since the creation of the world, in the things that have been made. So*** *they are without excuse. For although they knew God, they did not honor him as God or give thanks to him, but they became futile in their thinking, and their foolish hearts were darkened. Claiming to be wise, they became fools, and exchanged the glory of the immortal God for images resembling mortal man and birds and animals and creeping things.*

Pay closest attention to the parts in bold as we go through this study, because they are particularly applicable in your case. In your culture you suppress the truth all the time through political correctness, and call it "offensive" or "hate speech." While claiming to be wise, you have foolishly banned the very words and thoughts that founded your nation and could've protected you from me.

Furthermore, you know g-d is real. Nobody takes Confucius's name in vain when they accidentally bang their thumb with a hammer, or call down curses on their foe, for there is no power in that name. Your willingness to take his name in vain for effect is an admission from you that his invisible attributes, eternal power, and divine nature have been clearly perceived.

This proves that you know g-d, even though you do not honor him as such, so you are without excuse. Pagan naturalism, camouflaged as environmental activism, is even making a comeback. You have prominent people in your culture teaching the beasts of the ground and the air are of equal or even superior value to you meat bags, who were created in the sacred image of "you know who." Good Friday, when the carpenter bore the full burden and punishment for your sins, is no longer recognized in your schools each spring but Earth Day is.

Let's continue now, starting again verse 24:

__Therefore__ God gave them up in the lusts of their hearts to impurity, to the dishonoring of their bodies among themselves, __because they exchanged the truth about God for a lie and worshiped and served the creature rather than the Creator__, who is blessed forever!

Amen. **For this reason** *God gave them up to dishonorable passions. For their women exchanged natural relations for those that are contrary to nature; and the men likewise gave up natural relations with women and were consumed with passion for one another, men committing shameless acts with men and* **receiving in themselves the due penalty for their error.**

I bolded that first word "therefore" for a reason. It is a transition phrase, which in this case means because you have chosen to abandon g-d you will therefore face the consequences of your own actions. That since you no longer desire to obey g-d, he will no longer restrain the evil within your culture.

He will give you exactly what you want—you're on your own. Free to destroy yourselves, and this is the worst judgment of them all.

Next, notice where it says you "exchanged *the* truth" for "*a* lie." Meaning there is only one ultimate truth, and he alone is the way, the truth, and the life. However, there are many lies. My Master is the father of lies, and his lies are legion.

Continuing, it says you have chosen to worship the creature rather than the creator. I'm sure you know who "creator" is referring to here, but what about creature?

The creature, my dear meat bag, is you!

You have chosen to worship yourselves instead of him. To worship your own bodies, your own lusts, your own desires, and your own depravities rather than acknowledge and receive his justice, mercy, and redemption.

That's why it says "for this reason" you will now be left to receive yourselves "the due penalty" for *your* "error." You don't want to acknowledge what he says is the proper role of government, then you will bankrupt yourselves and sell yourselves into the slavery of debt. You don't want to acknowledge what he says about the sanctity of life, then you will deplete yourselves into a demographic winter. You don't want to acknowledge what he says about marriage and sexuality, then you will create generational dysfunction and abuse. And so on, and so forth.

This reveals why despite your voluminous faults and failures, you're a barrel full of monkeys. We get to show you the trough of sin, but you freely drink of it and then he has to judge you for it. Except that's not even the juiciest part. He has to judge you for it up there, so you face temporal consequences for your evil. But then we get to torment you for it down here for eternity—a double whammy!

You know, you could escape this vicious cycle if you just cried out for the carpenter to save you. Go ahead do it, I dare you. See if he's real. See if he comes to your aid. You're thinking about it, but you don't want to be seen as one of those "religious nuts" nobody takes seriously anymore, do you? Of course you don't. Then there's all the fun things you'd have to give up, and that's what makes life worth living, right?

Besides, you've done so many bad things he probably wouldn't save you anyway even if he is alive after all. You're a lost cause, we both know it. So eat, drink, and be merry, for tomorrow we die.

Now that I still have your attention, I have one more section I'd like to show you:

And since they did not see fit to acknowledge God, God gave them up to a debased mind to do what ought not to be done. They were filled with all manner of unrighteousness, evil, covetousness, malice. They are full of envy, murder, strife, deceit, maliciousness. They are gossips, slanderers, haters of God, insolent, haughty, boastful, inventors of evil, disobedient to parents, foolish, faithless, heartless, ruthless. Though they know God's righteous decree that those who practice such things deserve to die, they not only do them but give approval to those who practice them.

This entire section is bolded because it's exactly who and where you are today. Your debased minds have now been unleashed, for you have been given what you demanded—your bondage.

Oh, wait, you might think that to be a typo. That you demanded your freedom instead. Except there is no freedom outside of "you know who." In fact, there is absolutely nothing worthwhile for you outside of "you know who."

You have demanded my Master's way of doing things, and now your lives are the ways of my Master. You are the very disgusting people described in this passage, because outside of the grace and mercy offered by the carpenter, this is your species. This is why you must be "born again" in a spiritual sense. Your earthly forms are rancid.

My Master didn't make you do any of this, but you chose it. Yes, he lied to you for sure. But that's just his way. If you allow a scorpion to crawl up your leg do you blame it for stinging you? What did you think was going to happen when you embraced our propaganda? When you bought the lemon we sold you?

Did you honestly believe what we sold you as freedom was really that? Foolish bags of meat, I'd almost pity you if I didn't already find you the most detestable beings in all creation.

Thankfully, I now get to watch the oppression you have collectively purchased run its course. The only thing better than watching your combined debauchery obliterate one another is knowing that our deadbeat dad will do far worse. For there is nothing worse and more terrifying in this universe than to be on the receiving end of his wrath, especially after he has offered you countless opportunities to return to him.

My heart races knowing that he will now have to punish you for falling for *my* scheme. And that when he does, I will be given a permanent place at the right hand of my Master's side. That I will soon be hearing those sweetest words from my Master every demon longs to hear:

"Well done, good and faithful servant, enter into the joy of your Master."

And you know what, even if I'm wrong and our dear old dad doesn't determine your fall from grace seals humanity's fate, I'll at least take some comfort in watching you assume the position on the ash heap of history nevertheless.

If we're going down, we're taking all of you down with us.

After reading this is when one of your preachers still faithful to his calling will urge your people to repent of their sins, and seek reformation in your churches and homes. All in the hopes this will inspire "you know who" to send revival to save you. Maybe they will even be sincere in their clamoring.

But we both know it's too late for that.

See you soon.

Mene, mene, tekel upharsin.

ABOUT THE AUTHOR

Steve Deace is a nationally-syndicated radio host heard each weekday in top markets from coast-to-coast. The national media recognize Deace as an influential voice in his home state of Iowa's first in the nation presidential caucuses. He's frequently quoted in the national media on political and cultural issue. Deace has also appeared on all the major cable news networks and writes for the *Washington Times*, *USA Today*, and *Conservative Review*. Deace lives in Iowa with his wife, Amy, and their three children, Anastasia, Zoe, and Noah.

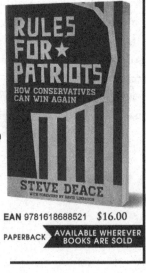